The Valerons - Honor Bound

Some things grab a man's attention . . . like being shot at! Jared Valeron learns that an unknown gunman has tarnished the Valeron reputation by killing a man while impersonating his cousin, Wyatt Valeron.

In trying to track down the culprit, Jared is drawn into an odd mystery at a gold-mining town. Solving the riddle of the killer's target requires discovering a motive for the murder. When his investigative efforts propel him deep into a hole, only his cousins can help dig him out. Before the folly ends, guns will be drawn and bullets will fly. Family honor sometime comes at a high price.

The Valerons - Honor Bound

Terrell L. Bowers

A Black Horse Western

ROBERT HALE

© Terrell L. Bowers 2020
First published in Great Britain 2020

ISBN 978-0-7198-3095-2

The Crowood Press
The Stable Block
Crowood Lane
Ramsbury
Marlborough
Wiltshire SN8 2HR

www.bhwesterns.com

Robert Hale is an imprint
of The Crowood Press

Typeset by
Derek Doyle & Associates, Shaw Heath
Printed and bound in Great Britain by
4Bind Ltd, Stevenage, SG1 2XT

CHAPTER ONE

Donny pushed his sister away, facing the sneering gunman alone. He wore his gun, but he had seldom shot at anything. It was more for show, and the fact that everyone other than the miners was armed.

'You've got the wrong man,' Donny said, fear nearly choking off his words. 'I'm no gunman.'

The dark-eyed stranger kept his hand over his own gun, ready to draw. With a sneer on his lips, he shook his head.

'You're the one I want, Donald Duval. Either reach for that smoke wagon or I'll kill you where you stand.'

Donny's voice rose an octave. 'But I don't even know you!'

'Name's Wyatt Valeron,' the man said calmly. 'And it's your time to die!'

Donny took a step back as the gunman began his draw. Knowing he was about to be shot in cold blood, he made a clumsy attempt to get his gun free of its holster. He was much too slow.

The stranger fired three times, each bullet hitting Donny in the chest. He slumped to the ground without so much as a groan.

Crystal screamed in horror, having witnessed her brother being gunned down before her eyes. She threw herself on the ground and cradled Donny's head on her lap. It was too late to help him; his eyes were vacant and staring at the sun. She rocked her brother back and forth. Agony ripped her heart to shreds as tears streamed from her eyes. She could only sob the question: 'Why? Why? Why?'

There was absolutely no reason for this cold-blooded murder. What did Wyatt Valeron have against her brother? Why would he shoot an innocent man in cold blood? It made no sense! No sense at all!

Sketcher, Shane Valeron, and the other four riders stopped at the crossroads.

'You sure you want to head up to Castle Point?' Sketcher asked Jared Valeron.

'Haven't seen Nash in a coon's age, Sketch. After driving another hundred steers to the railroad, I'm due a vacation.'

'Never figured you to be such a pampered girl,' his cousin Shane chuckled.

One of their cowhands, Amos, popped off with, 'Plain as day, Jared ain't used to actual hard work.'

'Right you are,' his pal, Johnson agreed. 'Hunting is his passion, 'cause it don't involve tending a bunch of head-strong steers.'

'OK, OK,' Jared put an end to the teasing. 'I get it. You men do the real work on the ranch, while I get a pass due to my supplying meat for the entire Valeron clan . . . and all of you smart-mouthed yahoos, too.' He snorted his humor. 'Maybe you'd prefer to have a steady diet of nothing but beef. No rabbit, sage hens, no venison, no buffalo?'

Shane laughed his surrender. 'All right, Jer. You've got a point.'

'Just dusting your hat, O Great Hunter,' Amos joined in. 'I, for one, admit that I do enjoy a change in menu. That wild turkey a few weeks back was durn special.'

'I had to scout up nearly a dozen of them to have enough for all of the hands,' Jared said. 'I can tell you, that was no easy chore. Turkeys don't travel in flocks of that size.'

'What're you going after this time?' Johnson wanted to know.

'Been a spell since we had any buffalo,' Jared replied. 'And I promised Reese a new hide. His old buffalo coat is practically bare – looks more like a flour sack these days.'

Shane stated, 'So, you intend to visit brother Nash, then head for the Dakotas?'

'There's still a couple herds up north. I'll try and get some meat before they cross the Canadian border.'

'Well, as much as I like bison, I have a family,' Sketcher said proudly. 'I wish you good luck and good hunting.'

The rest of the group voiced their agreement. As for Shane, he lifted a hand in farewell and said: 'You know where to reach us if you run into trouble, Cuz.'

'I'll be seeing you,' Jared replied. Then he turned his horse toward the town of Castle Point.

Mitch Winters had been trying to win Crystal's hand for several months. The romance had been like trying to get warmth from the moon. She allowed him to court her, but holding hands was the total affection he'd managed to this

7

point in time.

He stood in the doorway of the apartment – the one she and Donny had shared – with his hat in his hand, implanted like an iron gate.

'You can't do this, Crystal,' he stated firmly. 'It's not a chore for a genteel woman.' He uttered a minor profanity, and added: 'It's not a job for anyone, other than a gun-toting specialist. What are you gonna do – challenge and draw against Wyatt Valeron? He's about the most deadly man with a gun in the country!'

The young woman's chestnut-colored eyes glowed with determination. With her flaxen hair snugged in a bun atop her head, she placed Donny's riding hat on her head. 'This is none of your affair, Mitch,' she declared. 'I stood by and watched that murdering scum shoot Donny down like a diseased dog. He gave him no chance at all!'

'Yeah, but to try and. . . .'

'Are you going to lend me one of your rental horses, or do I have to steal one?!'

Mitch bit back his ire and attempted to reason with her. 'It's saddled and waiting, but give me a day or two to get my work caught up. I'll go with you. This is too much of a job for you to handle all by yourself.'

There was no give, no concession in her expression. 'I've made up my mind, Mitch. I can't . . . I won't rest until that filthy murderer is dead and buried!'

'It's sheer madness,' Mitch said gently. 'How will you even find Wyatt Valeron?'

'I'll find him, or one of his clan. I've seen stories of the Valerons in the Denver newspaper. I know where to look.'

'You're blinded by grief,' he pleaded. 'Let's send off some telegrams – at least track the man down before you simply ride. . . .'

'Get out of my way!' she cut him off. 'No one is going to stop me. This is something I have to do.'

'But, Crystal. . . .'

She strode forward and physically pushed him aside. Anything Mitch might have said after that, she didn't hear. Her mind was set. Every vestige of her being demanded she find and kill the man who had coldly and ruthlessly murdered her beloved brother.

Jared arrived in the small town of Castle Point in the late afternoon. He left his horse at the livery and proceeded over to Nash's house and office. Some new additions had taken place since his last visit, plus there was now a professionally painted sign out front that read 'Castle Point Clinic, Nash Valeron, MD'.

There were no patients when Jared entered the clinic. Nash's wife, Trina, heard the jingle of the bell on the door and came from the treatment room. Seeing him, she ran over to welcome him with a short, yet warm, hug.

'Jared!' she exclaimed, smiling as she backed up a step. 'We weren't expecting you.'

'Should have warned you not to get too close to me. I'm covered with a week's dust from a cattle drive. Sketcher was in such a hurry to get back to his family that we didn't even spend the night in Cheyenne. Some of the boys weren't too happy about that.'

'Jerry!' Nash offered up a smile, walking in to join the reunion. 'Good to see you, big brother.'

As the two of them shook hands, Trina moved next to Nash and locked her arm through his. It was as natural as most men donning their hat, and the act brought a smile to Jared's face.

'I hate to arrive without forewarning. I reckon the two of you are still on your honeymoon.'

'That's going to be a permanent state with us,' Nash responded, as he and Trina exchanged loving glances.

'OK, so I'm looking for an invite to a meal and a little catching up this evening. Will that be too much of an intrusion?'

Nash laughed. 'I think we can spare you a little time.'

'I'll get myself a room at the hotel and see about a bath. Packing all this dust, I don't want to contaminate your clinic.'

'Contaminate? There's a word I didn't know you knew, Jer,' Nash said. 'Did some of my studies actually rub off on you when we were together at the ranch?'

'Actually, I picked it up from a Texas drover. He told a tale about how longhorn cattle from down his way seemed to contaminate range cattle up through Kansas and the like.'

'Yes,' Nash said. 'I believe they tracked the source to a tick of some kind.'

'I'll inspect myself for ticks, while I'm at it, so you and Trina can feel safe.'

'Better get a move on,' Trina offered. 'It's nearly sundown.'

'Yeah, can't dally too long,' Nash put in. 'The wife usually has our evening meal ready at dusk.'

Jared grunted. 'Uh-huh, right. Unless someone shows up with a boil on their backside or a ready-to-be mother arrives with a baby seeking daylight for the first time. Then the evening meal might be served up at midnight.'

'Plan on dusk!' Trina stated with mocked sincerity. 'If

you're late, you'll be eating cold leftovers.'

Jared laughed and stepped out the door. The sun was touching the rolling hills on the western horizon as he began to cross the street. Suddenly, a voice yelled . . . 'Valeron!'

As he swung his attention in a westerly direction of the shout, partially blinded by the bright sun, a gunshot and muzzle-flash went off!

Simultaneously, a bullet screamed by his head, close enough it whistled past his ear!

In automatic response, Jared drew and fired before the attacker could get off a second shot. Though barely able to make out the assailant some sixty feet away, his shot was instantaneous with a cry of surprise and pain . . .

He saw the culprit sink to the ground as the echo of the shriek revealed the voice was not a man's cry . . . but that of a woman!

Hearing the gunshots, Nash rushed out from his clinic. He threw an alarmed look at Jared. 'What the heck's going on?'

But Jared called 'Come on!' and sprinted up the street. The two men arrived to discover a young woman lying on the ground. She was dressed in men's clothing, with a gunbelt and holster around her middle. Her long reddish-brown hair spilled out from beneath a weathered, western-style hat, and a Peacemaker Colt was lying at her side, inches from her right hand.

Nash squatted down next to the girl and quickly examined the wound. 'What's this about, Jerry?'

'I don't have any idea! I heard someone shout my name. I barely had a chance to look that direction when she fired off a shot at me. Didn't miss by more than an inch or two. I was half-blinded by the sun; I could hardly see the shooter. I fired back at a figure with a gun in their hand.'

'You recognize her?'

'Never seen her before,' Jared informed him. 'Is she hit bad?' With a naked fear in his voice, 'Tell me I haven't killed her!'

Nash expelled a sigh of relief. 'Appears your bullet went into the flesh below the collarbone. The bullet missed the vital organs.' He rocked back on to his heels. 'It doesn't look to be a mortal wound.'

'Thank You, Lord!' Jared exclaimed. 'I've never shot at a woman before.' He hurried to add, 'First time I ever had one shoot at me, too.'

Several people had gathered around, but Nash and Jared ignored their questions and carried the injured party to the exam room at Nash's clinic. As Nash explained the patient's condition, Trina scowled at Jared.

'Since when do you shoot down helpless women?'

'The sun was in Jerry's eyes, darling,' Nash defended his brother. 'The girl fired first and he didn't know she was a woman.'

'She's not much more than a child,' Trina observed. 'I doubt she's more than twenty years old.'

'Honest, Trina,' Jared continued to suffer from angst and regret. 'I haven't got the slightest idea who she is or why she tried to kill me.'

'Hot water and disinfectant,' Nash ordered his wife and nurse. 'I'll treat the bullet wound while she's unconscious. It looks to have lodged against her shoulder blade. Keep the chloroform handy in case she starts to wake up.'

Jared went through the young woman's pockets and

found a few coins and the name 'Wyatt Valeron' on a piece of paper. He informed Nash of the discovery.

'You said she called out your name?'

'The only word she shouted was 'Valeron' – then she opened fire.'

'Why shoot at you, if she was looking for Wyatt?' Nash wondered.

'Patch her up good and proper, little brother,' Jared replied. 'I'm as curious about the answer to that as you.'

CHAPTER TWO

Blinking against the early morning light coming through a small curtained window, the injured woman managed to focus her eyes on Trina. She attempted to lift her hand as a lock of auburn hair had draped over one of her chocolate-colored eyes. She stopped the movement and moaned from a sudden streak of pain. Before she could speak, Trina put a glass of water to her lips and gently lifted the back of her head enough so she could swallow.

'Take it easy,' she warned the young woman in a motherly voice. 'We don't want you to start bleeding again.'

The girl took several swallows, then pressed her lips together to show she had drank enough.

'The bullet had to be removed from your shoulder,' Trina advised her. 'You're fortunate to be alive. My husband doesn't think there will be any permanent damage.'

The girl moistened her lips with her tongue. 'Did I get him? Did I kill the man . . . Valeron?' she asked, unable to conceal the hopeful anticipation from her voice.

'Why on earth did you want to kill him?' Trina asked, not answering her question.

14

She literally seethed her words, 'That murdering scum, Wyatt Valeron, killed my brother!'

'The man you shot at was not Wyatt Valeron.'

She rolled her head back and forth. 'I couldn't find Wyatt. Someone told me this Valeron was his brother. I wanted to get even for what Wyatt did.'

'Jared is not Wyatt's brother; they are cousins.'

The talking of two men in the next room interrupted their conversation. Trina looked at the door and said, 'It sounds like Jared is back. My husband sent him to the store to get you a dressing gown. I'll be right back.'

The injured woman eased her head up to look around. She was in a small room with a single window and two beds. Her arm and shoulder felt like it was on fire, but she spotted her jacket, blouse and gunbelt hanging on a rack. The pistol had been put in the holster.

From the other side of the closed door, she could hear the three people talking in hushed tones. It was enough to cover the sound of her involuntary groan from swinging her legs over the side of the bunk. With her left hand pressed to the newly bandaged wound, she lurched over to the pile of clothes. Removing the gun, she cocked the hammer back and moved slowly to the door.

Taking a deep breath to fight the weakness of her knees, she used her left hand to take hold of the door handle. Even as she started to pull the door aside, Trina returned – and ran right into her. The abruptness of the collision knocked the gun from her hand and caused her to back-pedal a step to maintain her balance.

'Good gracious, girl!' Trina exclaimed, stepping forward to catch her. 'What do you think you're doing?'

The wounded patient folded at the middle with pain,

her weight almost dragging Trina to the floor. They would have both went down had not Jared arrived. He grabbed the girl about her waist and supported her in his arms.

'Easy there, little lady,' he tried to calm her. 'You'll undo all of the patchwork on your shoulder.'

'G-get your blood-soaked hands off of me!' she yelped like a stepped on cat. 'Let me go!'

But Jared muscled her over to the exam room table, lifted her up, and sat her down. She refused to lie back, sitting up and holding her right hand over her wound.

The girl wept and tears streaked down her cheeks. However, it was obvious the tears were more frustration than pain.

'Damn you, Valeron!' she hissed the words through her clenched teeth. 'Damn you and every killer with a gun!'

'Get out of here, Jerry!' Trina ordered. Then, with more composure: 'Please. This girl is going to do more harm to herself if she doesn't settle down!'

'I've got this, Jer,' Nash added. 'Best wait in the reception room.'

'Sure thing, little brother. I never was that fond of women anyhow – especially one who dresses like a man and keeps trying to kill me!'

Nash checked the girl's wound. Luckily, the bandage had held. There was a little blood showing, but the dressing didn't need to be changed.

'Stay with her, darling,' he told his wife. 'I'll make sure the patient's bed is ready for her.'

'Of course, dear,' Trina replied.

As soon as he had left the room, Trina glared at the patient. 'Are you crazy?' she wanted to know. 'You were nearly killed by a bullet not twelve hours ago and you're trying to shoot someone again!'

'Not someone,' the angry girl grated each word. 'A Valeron.'

'I'm a Valeron, too!' Trina announced curtly. 'And so is my husband. Do you intend to shoot all three of us?'

The news subdued the girl's rage. Even so, she did not relent. 'Just the man I missed. He's related to Wyatt, and Wyatt killed my brother.'

Trina frowned. 'When and where did this happen?'

'A little over a week ago, at the mining town of Quick-Silver, Colorado.'

'I've never heard of the place.'

The girl sighed, as if weary of answering questions. 'It's not very big, located about fifty miles from Boulder.'

'And this shooting took place a week ago?'

'Give or take a day.'

Trina shook her head. 'Wyatt Valeron couldn't have shot your brother, young lady. He got married last month. He and his wife made their home in the town of Valeron. They opened a hardware and gun shop there a couple weeks ago. I'm absolutely certain he hasn't left town since the wedding.'

A tight frown showed the girl didn't believe Trina.

'Did you actually see this man, the one you claim was Wyatt Valeron?'

'I stood helplessly by as he forced my brother into a gunfight. He said his name was Wyatt Valeron and he was going to kill Donny whether he defended himself or not. The man shot my brother three times before Donny could even get the gun out of his holster! It was cold-blooded murder!'

'I'm positive Wyatt would not do something like that.'

17

'Well, I was not five steps away when he shot my brother! He never gave him a chance!' She closed her eyes, suffering from the misery of the gunshot wound and the complete failure of her mission. 'No one could tell me where to find Wyatt, but I was told a Valeron lived in Castle Point. I had run out of money and had no way to travel any further – it's why I shot at the man in the next room.'

'Meaning you might have shot my husband?'

That brought the girl's fury to a halt. 'No. He is a doctor and doesn't carry a gun. The man at the livery told me another Valeron was in town, one known to have ridden with Wyatt many times.'

'Something is very wrong, young lady. Wyatt is not a cold-blooded killer, and Jared only fights when necessary.'

The girl shook her head. 'I'm not a dummy. I know what I heard and saw.'

'Wait here a minute,' Trina said. She then hurried from the room, returning a minute or two later with a newspaper in her hands. She held it out for the patient to look at.

'This is a picture of Wyatt and Jared – the photograph was in the Denver newspaper a year or so back. The two of them brought in three men wanted for several crimes, including murder.'

The girl squinted, peering intently at it. 'Can't hardly make out their faces.'

Trina then produced a sketching of a man and a woman in a romantic, cheek-to-cheek pose. 'How about this? One of the men working at the Valeron ranch is an exceptional artist. This is a wedding sketch he sent to us. We couldn't attend the ceremony so he drew this especially for Nash and me.'

She rolled her head slightly from side to side. 'That's

not Wyatt Valeron.'

'It is!' Trina vowed. 'The drawing is unbelievably lifelike. Sketcher is very talented and I swear to you: this is Wyatt Valeron. If you look closely, he and Jared do share many of the same features. They are as similar as Nash and Jerry.'

She studied the sketch. The man in the drawing was completely unlike the gunman who had killed her brother. This subject had strong, yet gentle features, and was much better looking than the thinly built, pock-faced assailant who had pushed Donny into a fight. Plus, the photograph in the newspaper was clear enough to recognize it was the same man as in the sketch. The girl frowned in confusion.

'But why would the killer use Wyatt Valeron's name?'

Jared, who had been covertly listening from the doorway to the waiting room, entered without invite and stopped with his arms folded. 'That, little lady,' he stated smartly, 'is exactly what you and I are going to find out!'

Her eyes widened and her mouth opened in alarm at seeing the man close up.

'As you were never properly introduced, this is Jared Valeron,' Trina presented him to the wounded girl. 'The man you tried to kill . . . twice!'

'I felt the breeze of the bullet go past my head,' Jared affirmed. 'If I hadn't turned out of the bullet's path to see who yelled out my name, you'd have hit me square.'

'I-I was sure the man was Wyatt Valeron,' she defended herself. 'Why would the killer pretend to be someone he wasn't?'

'My cousin has a reputation for speed and accuracy with a handgun,' Jared told her. 'His name would put fear in anyone who knew his reputation. But he's not in that line of work any longer.'

'Wyatt nearly died in a gunfight a short time back,' Trina filled in the details for the girl. 'The bullet went through his chest and he barely survived. Wyatt said it was nature's way of telling him it was time to hang up his gun . . . which he did.'

'Deserted me like a craven coward,' Jared complained. 'He and I shared a solemn pact – we weren't ever going to get hitched.' He grunted his displeasure. 'But he sure enough met his Delilah. If you looked at the picture Sketcher sent Nash and Trina, you can see his wife is a sly little fox with the beauty of an angel. She sucked him into the world of matrimony.'

'You didn't seem to mind my marrying your brother,' Trina issued a critical warning. 'Or do you also blame me for stealing Nash from your bachelors' club?'

Jared emitted a natural laugh. 'Quite the opposite, Trina. Nash has needed a wife to look after him since he was twelve. He was always too busy doctoring and studying to take care of himself. Wyatt and me. . . .' Another sigh. 'Well, we were going to grow old together.'

'Excuse me for butting in,' the patient complained. 'Just what did you mean – the two of us are going to find my brother's killer?'

'Soon as you can ride without doubling over in the saddle, we are going to track that murdering gutter rat down. No one gets away with impersonating my cousin. Especially a cold-blooded killer!'

'They do have buggies for transporting a lady about,' Trina reminded him. 'You can't expect a girl, recovering from a bullet wound, to travel on horseback.'

'Reckon we can make the journey the slow way,' Jared

20

changed his tune. 'Probably take the train from Cheyenne and get off at the stop nearest her home town.'

'We ought to know your name first,' Trina posed the query. 'Who do I tell my husband is the person who tried to kill his older brother?'

'I'm Crystal Duval,' she said. 'And . . . I'm sorry for trying to shoot you.'

'You need to describe every detail about how the shooting of your brother came about,' Jared announced. 'If we're going to get this guy, we have to. . . .'

'Not right now!' Trina stopped him cold. 'This poor girl needs plenty of liquids and lots of rest. Isn't it enough that you shot the poor child?'

Jared back-pedaled a step. 'But she shot at me first, Trina. And I didn't know she was a woman!'

'Out!' she ordered, flipping the back of her hands in his direction, shooing him like an unwanted pet. 'Leave her be.' With a scolding tone, 'You can start your inquisition when she is feeling stronger.'

'Inquisition?' Jared's voice rose several octaves. 'She tried to kill me!'

'Out!' Trina was insistent. 'I'll tell you when you can see her. Get out, so she can recover from the damage done by your bullet!'

Throwing his hands into the air in complete frustration, Jared whirled about and left the room.

'It was my fault,' Crystal murmured, after he had left. 'I almost killed a completely innocent man.'

Trina smiled. 'Trust me . . . Jared isn't all that innocent.'

The following day, Nash inspected the young lady's wound and was satisfied there was no infection. He then replaced the dressing and pulled Crystal's hospital gown back up in place.

'How does it feel today?' he asked.

'It throbs whenever I move,' she replied. 'Long as I stay still, it's bearable.'

'You were lucky. Being only about five feet in height and having the sun at your back saved your life. Jerry is very good with a gun. A couple inches taller and he would have killed you.'

'I thought . . .' but she couldn't rationalize the hate and resolve she had been living with since watching her brother die before her eyes. 'It was a mistake,' she finished weakly.

'You couldn't possibly know how much of a mistake,' he told her quietly. 'Jerry is very much a protector of women and children, women of all ages − family and strangers alike. He grew up watching out for all of the Valeron girls, and he's never failed to step in whenever a woman or child was being abused or threatened. Of all the men I've ever known, Jerry is the one man I would trust to take care of my wife, sister, mother or daughter. If he had killed you by mistake . . . it would have destroyed him.'

'Trina told me about how he saved her from a couple of bounty hunter types when she first came here.'

'On that one occasion he didn't even know Trina was in the room,' Nash clarified. 'One of those men poked our sister with his finger.' With a grin, 'Big mistake.'

'I see.'

'However, Jerry did help win Trina's freedom. He also hanged three men who kidnapped Scarlet, our older sister. If Brett − our brother who carries a US Marshal's badge – hadn't covered for him, a judge might have seen Jerry's actions as that of a vigilante.'

'Kidnapping is a hanging offense,' Crystal said, defending the deed.

'Yes, after a trial,' Nash replied. 'But Jerry didn't wait. Those men had grabbed and terrified our sister. They killed her husband-to-be in front of her eyes. Every breath they took was an offense to him.' He looked her directly in the eyes. 'That's why he won't hold what you tried to do against you. He knows the terrible hurt and rage that fills a body when someone they love is harmed.'

'He . . . he said he was going to take me back to Quick-Silver and learn the identity of the man who pretended to be Wyatt Valeron.' She lowered her eyes. 'I . . . I must admit, I am ashamed for trying to kill him. I don't know if I can face being alone with him.'

'Well, that's why I wanted to explain about his passion for justice.'

'You mean revenge.'

'No. Yours was an act of revenge – attempting to kill someone besides the guilty party to get even. Justice and revenge are two sides of the same coin when going after the guilty person, the one responsible for the deed.'

'I ran out of time and money, I couldn't find the man I was looking for,' Crystal admitted quietly.

Nash smiled. 'If you had tracked down cousin Wyatt, you would have recognized that he wasn't the man for whom you were searching.'

Crystal shifted her weight and grimaced. 'I wish I had found him instead of your brother – it would have saved me getting shot.'

'Jerry will get to the bottom of it,' Nash professed. 'He's

a mule with the bit between his teeth once he goes after someone.'

'I want to believe you.'

'There had to be a reason for such a conspicuous murder,' Nash said. 'Jerry's theory is that someone hired a gunman to eliminate your brother. It's the only thing that makes sense. Donny must have either done, seen, or discovered something that got him killed.'

'And Jared believes he can find the truth by himself?'

'No.' Nash grinned. 'It's why he is waiting for you to heal enough to make the trip to Quick-Silver. When I spoke with him last night, he said you were the key to discovering the truth behind why your brother was killed.'

'But I don't know. . . .'

Nash raised a hand to stop her protest. 'It is probably something you haven't thought of, maybe a clue or fact that has not entered your mind yet. The trauma of watching someone you love die . . . it doesn't allow a person to think clearly. Add to the tragedy your desire for retribution and being shot – you've had little time to concentrate on anything else.'

Crystal moistened her lips with her tongue and frowned thoughtfully as she considered his logic.

'If you feel up to it today, try a short walk around the room now and again. Exercise will help the body recover from the shock of being wounded. Tomorrow or the next day, we'll have you start taking walks outside. One of us will accompany you until you get your strength back.'

'You've been very good to me, Doctor Valeron.' She sighed. 'Especially when it was your brother I tried to kill.'

Nash joked, 'It's not the way I would have recommended getting Jer's attention, but it worked.'

Crystal laughed shortly. 'I think I'll try a tap on his shoulder the next time.'

CHAPTER THREE

Andrew Lariquett stood at the window and watched Sylvia
Adour walk alongside her much older sister-in-law, making
their way from Jacques Adour's business toward their
home a short way down the street. Even from such a distance, he was infused with the warmth of desire, a craving
from which he had suffered since the first moment he laid
eyes on the woman.

He mentally cursed himself for the mistake he had
made. Being sought after by numerous women, hand-
some, outwardly possessing wealth and power, he had let
his ego get the best of him. It had been a mistake, and it
ended up costing the life of an innocent man.

Not that he lost much sleep over Donny Duval's death,
other than adding an inconvenience to his bookkeeping.
But it had hurt his relationship with Sylvia. She had
accepted his apology, but incurred her distrust and revul-
sion. She avoided him at all times, and were it not for his
threat to kill her husband, she might have ruined his life.

He again cursed his loss of impulse. What mattered to
him most was the loss of being close to her, hearing her
voice, and watching her move with all the grace and poise

of royalty. His teeth were anchored tightly as he battled against the memory of touching her soft flesh. He had almost realized his dream to possess her . . .

A tap at the door turned his head. Rizzo Nobb, his friend and trusted number one man, entered the room. He seldom knocked and never awaited a response. If Lariquett required privacy, it was necessary to throw the bolt and lock the door.

'What is it?' he asked the man.

'Seen you was at the window, Chief,' Rizzo replied. He was the only one in town who addressed Andrew Lariquett by a moniker other than Mister or Boss. 'Thought you might want to know – Parker got a query about Donny's death.'

'Yeah? From who?'

'Some fella named Valeron, over at Castle Point, Wyoming.'

'What did he want to know?' he asked, barely interested.

'Just the details of the shootout.'

'And what does Parker want from me?'

'He asked if you wanted him to reply to the wire. You know Parker – rogue that he is, he knows not to cross us. You OK with him answering the guy?'

Lariquett lifted his shoulders in a shrug. 'Nothing special about it; Donny perished when he was killed in a gunfight.'

'Gotta wonder, Chief,' Rizzo continued to worry. 'Why is some joker from a hundred miles away asking about Donny?'

Lariquett frowned. 'Wait. Did you say the telegram was from someone named Valeron?' At Rizzo's nod, he went on. 'Didn't your pal tell Donny and his sister that his name was Valeron?'

Rizzo slapped his forehead. 'You're right! Sutter claimed to be Wyatt Valeron. Most everyone has heard of him.'

'Now this gent is. . . .' Lariquett experienced a rush of anger. 'Damn it all! The last thing we need is a Valeron asking questions about this!'

Rizzo also swore. 'Gotta tell you, Chief. I didn't know Sutter was dumb enough to use the name of a town-taming legend like Wyatt Valeron. If this is one of his kin, we're liable to have a Valeron on our doorstep in the next day or two.'

'Have Parker wire back that no one is certain as to the name of the shooter. Only Donny's sister was close enough to hear what was said before the gunfight. As far as we know, the man was a total stranger to everyone in town.'

'Good thinking, Chief. I'll take care of it.'

Trina entered Crystal's room with a man at her side. She introduced him as Sketcher. He appeared quite ordinary, but had a compassionate quality and easy manner. The first words out of his mouth were, 'I'm so very sorry about your brother, Miss Duval. The trauma must be giving you endless nightmares.'

'I showed Crystal the wedding picture you sent us,' Trina explained what was going on. 'It was Jerry's idea that perhaps Sketcher could draw the man you saw.'

'Do what?'

'I've never tried this kind of thing,' Sketcher admitted. 'However, if I can draw a good enough likeness of the killer, Jared believes it will make his search much easier.'

28

Crystal stared at him dumbly. 'You want me to describe someone you've never seen and make a good enough likeness to identify him?'

'It's done on a good many wanted posters,' Sketcher informed her. 'The artists who draw those criminals have seldom actually seen them. The likeness is overseen by a person who provides the features needed, unless a photograph is available.'

'And Jared believes you and I can do this?'

Sketcher grunted. 'If not, I'll be very unhappy. I left my wife and four children to ride all the way here. I'd hate to think it was for nothing.'

Trina said,' I'll leave you two alone. Would you like anything, Sketch?'

'A glass of water would be good,' he replied. 'This may take some time.'

'How about you, Crystal?'

'I have the glass on the table, but I'll need to sit up. I won't be able to see his handiwork while lying down.'

Trina provided her with a couple extra pillows to prop her up, while Sketcher got his drawing material ready and positioned the chair next to the bed. Soon as they were both comfortable, the chore began.

'Now,' Sketcher said gently, 'I hate to put you through this, but I need for you to close your eyes. This will be painful, but you must get a good mental picture of the shooter. We'll start with his headgear and move downward, his hair, the shape of his face, his ears. Once we have an outline, you can concentrate on his features – eyebrows, nose, chin, mouth. We'll take it slow and change anything that isn't right. When I finish, I want you to be able to tell Jared that the drawing is accurate.'

'I'll do my best,' Crystal promised.

'All right,' Sketcher coaxed. 'Once you have his image clear in your mind, open your eyes and we'll begin.'

From the next room, Jared, Nash and Trina sat impatiently at the dinner table. It was early afternoon, no patients had come to the clinic, so there was little to do. Jared had a deck of cards, but no one was in a mood to play.

'Do you really believe Sketcher can do this?' Trina asked Jared. 'I mean, it's been over a week since the girl witnessed the shooting.'

'Remember back to when you were being held at the lunatic asylum?' he asked. 'I'll bet you can picture the doctor, nurse and every one of those inmates.'

'Yes, but I saw them every day. This girl only saw the killer once, and it was a horrid, terrible thing to see.'

'She only has to get close enough to make him recognizable. The man was a complete stranger to her and he left town right after killing her brother. Without a name or other information about the guy, I won't have a clue as to who I'm looking for.'

Nash rested his hands on the table and ducked his head. 'I sure hope this works. Sketcher barely got back to his family before you summoned him here. I can't imagine leaving a wife and four kids for a week, then being called away again.'

'I couldn't think of another way,' Jared said. 'This young lady about got herself killed trying to find the man who shot her brother. She became so desperate, she tried to kill anyone related to him.'

'Yes,' Trina said softly, 'the pain and grief has tore that poor girl's heart to shreds.'

'I'm going to find who did this,' Jared avowed. 'The telegraph message basically told us nothing. Actually, it was less than nothing, because the message said no one else heard the shooter call himself Wyatt Valeron.'

'Well,' Nash said, 'the girl was sure enough to come looking for any Valeron she could find. I doubt she would have undertaken such a vendetta unless she was absolutely certain of the name she heard.'

Jared outlined, 'First order of business is to find out who ordered her brother killed. No man assumes a false identity and simply kills an innocent bookkeeper for the fun of it. There's a mystery to be solved, and I intend to help the girl get to the bottom of it.'

'A mining town without any law,' Nash pointed out. 'You are going to need some help.'

'Once I figure out the who and the why of this, I'll know if I need help. Could be, someone had a grudge against Donny. It might be as simple as a rejected boyfriend, someone who thought Donny got between him and a girl.'

'And it might be something a whole lot bigger,' Nash warned.

Jared rocked back in his chair and grinned. 'Only time will tell, little brother. Only time will tell.'

Sketcher stayed the one night and was gone before day-light, in a hurry to get back to the ranch and his family. Shortly after breakfast, Nash and Trina were about to take Crystal for her first walk around town. That notion was put on hold when a patient arrived with a swollen jaw and an infected tooth.

Jared had nothing else to do so he volunteered to escort the young woman. She had been weakened by the

31

loss of blood and her poor overall condition. Hardly any sleep and very little food, while spending a week on the trail, meant she had lost several pounds and had barely acquired her appetite back. Being fragile and weak, she was forced to link her arm through Jared's for support.

'I didn't want to pry,' Crystal said, 'but Sketcher seems quite young to have four children.'

Jared relayed to her how Sketcher had come to the Valeron family as an orphan and explained the story of how he met his wife, and how they took four street children to join their family.

'He is an exceptional artist. The drawing of my brother's killer is near perfection.'

'Never seen anyone else who can sketch the way he can,' Jared agreed.

'This seems a most bizarre situation,' Crystal spoke again, after a short way. 'I mean, I try to kill you, and you are helping me to recover.'

'My mother warned me that women could be unpredictable at times,' Jared said with a grin.

'We are not talking a change of moods,' Crystal was stolid. 'I shot at you with the intent of killing you.'

'Other than for my sisters, I was never all that popular with girls,' he dismissed her concern.

'Why do you think that is?'

'Probably the fact I enjoy solitary living,' he replied. 'I've always loved to fish and hunt. Being out in the wilderness, under God's majestic sky, where it's peaceful and quiet . . . that's my kind of life.' He heaved a sigh. 'I reckon if I ever have an accident when I'm off alone, I'll likely die before anyone can find me.'

'That's a gruesome thought.'

'Civilization is taking over the country, Miss Duval. One day, it'll be so crowded and noisy, a person won't be able to get off by themselves and enjoy a serene moment. The wild game will be gone, like most of the buffalo. A great many of the wild horse herds have ceased to exist, too. Nope, I won't be around to see it, but the signs are as plain as the morning sun: people will one day cover every square inch of this country.'

Crystal felt the corners of her mouth lift in mirth. 'You know, I've never heard anyone use the word serene before. I've seen it in a book or two, but you're the first man I ever heard put it into a sentence.'

'Guess that shows what a rare breed of man I am,' he cracked.

Crystal did not comment on his theory, she completely changed the subject. 'Trina said you are a protector of the weak and helpless. She made you sound like some kind of dashing knight on a big white horse from a fairy tale.'

'I prefer chestnut, sorrel and dark colors for my steed,' he joked. 'Easier to blend in with the trees and brush.'

Crystal cocked her head enough to see the simper on his face. Unfortunately, she happened to step into a shallow dip on the street at the same time. The slight jar caused her to fall against him for support, due to the sudden jolt of pain.

Jared quickly wrapped his other arm around her and held her close until the pain subsided.

After a few seconds, Crystal let out a 'whew!' and removed herself from the unpremeditated embrace. Her coloring had a pink hue, obviously embarrassed over ending up in a strange man's arms. To cover the reaction, she said, 'Best keep my mind and eyes on where we are going. I'm not ready to jump any ditches just yet.'

'What say we wander over to the general store?' Jared offered. 'You can pick out an outfit for traveling back to Quick-Silver. Most people aren't keen about a young lady wearing men's clothes, and you can't wear a hospital gown and robe . . . it would be unladylike.'

'I'm completely broke. Even the horse and saddle I rode here are borrowed. I don't have the money to. . . .'

'It's not just for you,' Jared said quickly. 'It's to keep me out of trouble.' He lifted a careless shoulder. 'After what my sister-in-law told you, I'd be compelled to defend your honor every time someone spouted off about your wearing men's clothes or looking like a vagrant. If that happened with some frequency, we might never get you home.'

'But the cost of. . . ?'

He cut her off in mid-sentence. 'Me and Wyatt rounded up several desperadoes who had bounties on their heads a while back. We sent all of the money to Nash, so he could improve and operate his clinic. He can afford a few bucks charged to his account.'

The storekeeper was at the counter when the two of them entered. He flashed a crooked grin. 'I couldn't believe it when I heard you had shot a woman, Jared. From what I've heard of your hunting prowess, you never shoot a doe or fawn.'

Jared flashed a good-natured grin. 'Well, none of those critters ever took a shot at me first, Cal. Another inch to the right and you'd be teasing the young lady here about killing the wrong man.'

'Enough joshing,' the man's wife interjected, coming in from the next room. 'Tell me you've come to get a decent outfit for this poor unfortunate girl. She can't be seen wearing a man's clothing – shouldn't be out in public exercising in a hospital gown and robe either.'

'I'm in full agreement,' Jared was in accord. 'It's why we're here.'

'I'm Cal's wife – Judy,' the woman introduced herself to Crystal. 'Tell me what all you need, honey.'

'I'd like a hundred .44-40 cartridges for my gun,' Crystal named off the first item of importance. 'It's obvious I need more practice.'

Jared frowned. 'You do know I'm going to find out who is behind the murder of your brother. I don't think. . . .'

'It's best if you don't try and talk me out of this!' Crystal took an obstinate posture. 'I'm going to be there with you. . . .' With a callous declaration: 'Or I'll be there without you.'

'Sure thing, little lady,' he didn't argue the point. 'I figured to let you back me up. But we can't charge in like an enraged grizzly. We have to find out who hired the man that killed your brother, and then we take them both down.'

Crystal's face displayed a complacent simper. 'I'm glad we're in accord, Mr Valeron,' she said. 'How-some-whatsoever, I missed you from fifteen steps away. I obviously need more practice.'

The storekeeper laughed. 'Trina warned us the lady had some grit.'

'Yeah,' Jared groaned. 'And a wit to match.'

'Cal, you set the ammunition on the counter,' his wife instructed. 'I'll take the lady to the back room so she can try on some clothing. I reckon she is going to need a full outfit for the trip home.'

'Yes,' Crystal agreed. 'I put on my brother's gun and clothes when I set out to find the man who killed him. I need most everything, including shoes. These are Mrs Valeron's slippers I'm wearing.'

Jared moved aside to uncouple their locked arms, while keeping an eye on her to make sure she was steady enough to maneuver on her own.

Crystal smiled at his concern. 'I'm fine,' she assured him. 'This nice lady can pick me up if I fall on my face.'

Jared watched her take a few steps without incident and then turned to the store owner. 'Better make that two hundred rounds of ammo,' he said, showing a dour acceptance of the situation. 'I'm going to be doing some practising too.'

CHAPTER FOUR

Mitch stopped working at the forge at Rizzo's entrance. He took off his gloves, set them aside, and moved over to see what he wanted. The man held out a piece of paper in his hand for Mitch to take.

'What's this?' he asked Lariquett's top gun-hand.

'It come for you whilst I was passing by Parker's place. He asked if I could deliver it for him. Seems the town runner was off on an errand.'

'I appreciate you taking the time,' Mitch said.

'Looks as if your gal is coming back,' he said, indicating the news he had brought. 'Bet you've been lying awake nights wondering where she was at.'

Mitch scanned the telegraph message. 'Due here in two or three days.' He frowned. 'But she's coming by rail. Wonder what happened to the horse and tack she borrowed?'

Rizzo chuckled. 'Probably sold them to buy her railroad fare. Being one of her suitors, you likely figured you wouldn't expect to get the saddle and horse back anyway.'

Mitch forced a grin. 'I reckon we men often get taken advantage of by women.'

'Didn't say anything about the success of her mission. I heard she left hell bent on finding the man who killed her brother.'

'Guess we'll have to wait and see,' Mitch replied. 'Maybe she gave up the quest. It sure ain't a job for a proper young woman.'

'Keogh said she left wearing men's duds when she left town. Never figured her for being that much of a tomboy.'

'She didn't have any riding outfits,' Mitch defended her. 'I admit, the pain and anger ate her up. I tried to talk to her, but she was beyond reaching. If I hadn't lent her a horse, I believe she'd have started walking.'

Rizzo snickered. 'Be glad to have her back. There ain't but two or three decent-looking women in town. Even though she is headstrong and temperamental, she's easy on the eyes.'

Mitch didn't reply, and Rizzo whirled about and wandered off in the direction of the saloon.

'What did he want?' Toby came up from the stalls to ask his older brother.

'You remember me telling you how Crystal borrowed a horse and tack from us?' Mitch reminded him. 'She sent this here telegraph message to tell me she was on her way home.'

'Think she got the job done?'

'I don't know, Tobe. She was more determined than anyone I ever seen. When I tried to reason with her, she got downright scary.'

'What's she gonna do? You think old man Baker will let her live upstairs for the little amount of help he needs?'

'Again . . . I don't know.'

'You could ask her to marry you?'

Mitch scoffed at the idea. 'She's allowed me to dance with her and hold hands a time or two, but there's other gents around who can make the same claim. I'm not certain I'm even in the running for her hand.'

'Being alone now, it might be the best offer she has on the table.'

'I got to finish welding that bracket,' Mitch got back to their work. 'How's the single-tree coming?'

Toby skewed his face in thought. 'Give me a while longer and it'll be ready to add the link.'

'Let's get to it then,' Mitch said, trying hard to slow the beat of his heart. Toby went back to his chore, while Mitch felt a tingle of apprehension.

Finally, he thought to himself, Crystal's coming home! At last!

Rather than take the stage from Castle Point, which was always a rough and jarring ride, Nash insisted Jared take his doctor's buggy. He had recently purchased a one-horse carriage with cushioned seats and canopy. With the help of the local blacksmith, the front seat had been divided so one side could fold down into a makeshift bed. It was functional to accommodate either a second person or a patient lying down when necessary. The ride would be more comfortable for Crystal, albeit a much slower trip to Cheyenne. From there, they could take the train.

Jared had discussed the schedules and route with Crystal. She explained they would be able to connect with the narrow gauge railroad spur from Boulder, which went all the way to Quick-Silver and back daily. Nash arranged for a man who owed him some money to make the eight-to-ten hour trip with them to Cheyenne. He would ride Jared's horse and return the carriage and extra horse back to Castle Point.

Crystal managed the first few hours sitting upright, but the constant jarring finally caused her to allow Jared to lower the seat so she could lay down. She took a sip of laudanum a time or two for the pain and was exhausted by the time they reached Cheyenne.

The fellow who had journeyed with them was spending the night at a friend's house, so he put up Jared's horse and took care of the carriage. Jared carried the luggage and escorted Crystal to a hotel he had used several times before. The girl had a pallor to her complexion and appeared too weary to visit a restaurant, so Jared accompanied her to a room so she could rest.

He then visited a dining establishment and ordered two dinners prepared, both made ready on a tray, with a cloth to keep the food warm. He arrived at the hotel to discover Crystal had removed her traveling clothes and donned her sleeping gown. For modesty sake, she also wore a robe as she rested atop the bed covers.

'You didn't have to go to so much trouble,' she told Jared, as he entered the room. 'I'm strong enough to have walked to a place to eat.'

He set the tray on the nightstand and then waited at the edge of her bed. 'Nash said to baby you some. No one bounces back from a gunshot wound overnight.'

'It's been several days,' she made no excuse, grimacing as she managed to sit up and scoot back to place her back against the headboard. 'And we did walk out of Castle Point far enough to practice shooting. That was, what? Three times. I should be about recovered.'

40

'Those outings were about an hour each,' Jared countered. 'All day being bounced around in a carriage is a whole different kind of exercise.'

A pert little frown came to her face. 'Yes, but the wound is healed over.'

'A gunshot isn't like having a cold,' he reminded her. 'And even that takes a couple weeks to shake off.'

'Your brother did a very professional job,' she persisted. 'There's been no bleeding . . . I no longer need to wear a bandage.'

'He's the best,' Jared praised, 'but a person's body balks at having a piece of hot lead going through it. You've probably still got some internal mending to do.'

He transferred his food to the night stand and placed the tray on her lap. Then, sitting on the room's single chair, the two of them began to consume the meal. They shared only a snip or two of small talk as they ate. When finished, Jared got to his feet, placed the dishes on the tray, and started to leave.

'Are you coming back to my room?' she asked. 'Do we need to discuss tomorrow's travel?'

'No. You need to get as much rest as you can for the train ride to Boulder. It won't be as rough as the carriage, but the benches are pretty hard.' He rotated about and reached for the door.

'Jerry?' she stopped him a second time.

He swung about, curious she had called him by his first name. There was also an unfathomable look on her face. Not exactly a frown, yet it appeared something was on her mind. He waited, allowing her to choose the words she wanted.

'Are you doing all of this simply to clear your cousin's

41

good name?'

The question sounded straightforward, yet this was a woman. It reminded him of times when his sisters would ask how he liked their new hairstyle or outfit. Usually, they were looking for more than a blanket approval – it's just the way the mind of some girls seemed to work. His married brothers had all impressed on him that, unlike most men, women didn't think in a continuous line.

Her brows arched in puzzlement. 'Is that such a hard question?'

'Uh, well,' he labored to decide on a proper response. 'What do you think?'

'I think it was a very simple question.'

'Miss Duval, I'm afraid I don't have a simple answer.'

'You're here!' she stated flatly. 'I'm asking you to tell me why!'

'Family honor, I suppose,' Jared squeaked out the reply.

'Was that so hard?' The girl's brows narrowed with a trace of ire. 'I mean, if you're thinking I am being coy, or curious as to what you might think of me. . . .'

Jared kept the tray balanced in one hand and held up the other. 'Whoa, lady!' he exclaimed, trying to get out of the room with his hide intact. 'Don't get a knot in your britches. I told you right off that I don't spend a lot of time around women – other than those I'm related to. I don't know the rules of engagement.'

'Rules of engagement!' she screeched. 'I'm not trying to have a battle with you. It was a straightforward question.'

'If you say so.'

'It's not as if I was asking if you found me attractive or had a notion about trying to woo or impress me. I merely asked if your only reason for being here is because of your cousin's reputation.'

He opened the door and sought a way to make an exit without showing manifest cowardice.

'Well?' the stern tone of her voice warned she intended to get an answer.

'I better get some rest, too!' Jared blurted out the words. 'The train leaves early and we won't have time for breakfast.'

She glared at him. 'Jared Valeron, you are a chicken-hearted, irritating, inconsiderate dolt!'

'Reckon you got me pegged, little lady.' he agreed. 'I'll wake you in time to get ready in the morning.' Then he escaped the room and quickly closed the door behind him.

As he found his way back to the street, he paused to gaze heavenward. 'Gotta wonder, Lord. Us men do thank you for making females so desirable and pretty, but did you have to make them so durned complicated?'

The train ride was easier on Crystal, but the pain increased enough that she still had to take a sip of laudanum. By the time they arrived in Boulder, Jared did not consider making the remainder of the journey until she had a full day to recuperate.

After a night at a hotel and having breakfast with the lady, Jared ordered her a bath and allowed she should rest up until lunch. For himself, he sought out the local law.

Boulder, Colorado, was a fair-sized city, home to a university and growing bigger and more modern all the time. The city had a courthouse and jail, with a number of police to enforce the laws and keep the peace. Almost no one carried a gun, other than a few travelers or hunters passing through.

Jared sat down with one of the officers who had been around town the longest. His name was Mylan Kochever, a fellow with a contented paunch from too many hours idle – plus a wife who knew how to cook. His hair had mostly turned gray, with sideburns that joined a neatly trimmed beard, minus a mustache.

'I met your brother once,' Mylan informed Jared. 'We attended a meeting in Denver together a few years back. It was a joint law enforcement meeting concerning counterfeit monies, presented by the Treasury Department, that sort of thing.'

'Brett busted up a big counterfeit ring about that time,' Jared recalled.

'We had a couple back-room printers who tried it in Boulder, but nothing of any size.'

'Why I'm here, Mylan,' Jared began – and he filled him in on Crystal's story and their trip back to find the people responsible. Next, he showed the lawman the drawing.

'This here is the fella I'm looking for.'

Mylan studied the sketch for a few seconds. 'Don't recognize him. Is this a good likeness?'

'The victim's sister swore it was equal to a photograph.'

'If the gent came through here, it was likely only long enough to board the train.'

Jared nodded. 'It isn't much to go on, but it's all I have.'

'Quick-Silver,' Mylan said meaningfully. 'Tough place. Not a lot of law up there. Some range land for the cattlemen and the mine, for which the town was named. Two men pretty much run the place – the mine owner and a guy who runs the biggest saloon in town. Jacques Adour is the gray-back bull of the herd. He owns the mine and most everything else. Andrew Lariquett – his hair's as white as mine, except it's been that way since he was a youngster – he runs the casino and bar operation.'

'The lady told me her brother worked for Lariquett as a bookkeeper and money handler. Considering he wasn't involved with a woman and had no enemies, she has no idea why he was the target of this unknown gunman.'

'Shows how little news comes down from there,' Mylan said. 'We never got notice of his death, but then we seldom get word of any gunfights or killings up at Quick-Silver.'

Jared gave him an educated look. 'I reckon that means I'm pretty much on my own.'

The lawman uttered a helpless sigh. 'Sorry, Valeron, but that's the truth of it; we've no jurisdiction up there. Your best bet is to keep someone like your brother informed. Brett being a US Marshal, his authority is about the only back-up you'll have.'

The ride on the narrow gauge railway lacked what little comfort there had been on the Union Pacific line, taxing Crystal's fragile state. Jared carried their luggage and accompanied her directly to her apartment. It was a three-room affair atop a hardware store, accessed by a flight of stairs at the rear of the building. The owner was an elderly man named Baker, who resided downstairs at the rear of his shop.

The door had a simple lock and Crystal remarked the place appeared untouched since Donny's death. It was clean, sparsely furnished, with a main living area that afforded a counter, a wash-pan and a couple of small cupboards for the dishware. A flat-topped stove provided heat

45

and a surface for cooking simple meals. A little round table had a tablecloth and two stools for dining. The only sitting area offered two cushioned chairs. Two closet-sized bedrooms had been partitioned off to make the apartment complete.

'Cosy den for the two of you,' Jared observed, as Crystal went over to one of the chairs and sank down. Her features were drawn from travel, but she smiled at his remark.

'Donny earned a decent wage, but the only work I could find was to help Mr Baker downstairs a couple days a week. I cleaned and helped stock his store.' Another smile. 'He is a nice man who says he's always been sorry he didn't take up baking, rather than having a hardware store . . . because of his last name.'

Jared chuckled. 'I can see why . . . Baker's Bakery would certainly garner attention.'

Crystal turned serious. 'So now what, Mr Valeron? How do we find out the who and why someone ordered my brother to be killed?'

Jared flinched at her calling him Mister. Thinking back, his refusal to answer her question about why he was helping her might be the reason. She had actually called him Jerry before that encounter. He didn't fully understand why, but the change from friendly to professional caused an uncomfortable pang somewhere deep within his chest.

'You said your brother was the bookkeeper and counted money for the saloon owner?' he confirmed, dismissing the discomfort.

'Yes, Andrew Lariquett runs the casino. His head overseer, a man named Rizzo, has a couple of men who keep order in town.'

46

'And Lariquett is a partner with the mine owner, Jacques Adour.' He spoke generally, confirming her information. 'Tell me about the two men – either of them married?'

'Jacques has a lovely wife. Sylvia dresses in the finest gowns and her sister-in-law or other escort accompanies her whenever she is out and about. I'd guess she is maybe half his age. Jacques looks to be about fifty, has little hair and is not much to look at. Andrew, on the other hand, has unusually white hair, but is probably fifteen years younger than Jacques. He also thinks of himself as something of a lady's man.' She uttered a feminine grunt. 'Donny warned me to stay away from him. Said the man was a hound around women, and he was afraid Lariquett might take an interest in me.'

'Probably concerned Lariquett might try and blackmail you into a relationship to protect your brother's job.' Jared snorted his contempt. 'I know the sort. Spent two weeks in jail for dealing with one such type a few years back.'

'To defend a lady friend?'

He could see she was trying to form a conclusion about the tale. Rather than dramatize the situation to test her true interests in him, he went with the truth.

'Actually, I never met the woman herself; she was one of my cousin Lana's friends. I convinced the lecher to leave Lana's friend alone. Got me a little jail time for breaking his nose, and, in the end, it didn't really do much good. The guy ended up in prison a year later for assaulting another woman. Goes to show lowlife perverts seldom change their ways, only their victims.'

'Those are the men you hate,' Crystal declared. 'I

remember Trina telling me you're in the habit of being a self-proclaimed protector of women.'

He couldn't tell if she was making fun of him or praising him, but he heaved his shoulders in a shrug. 'Some men have no respect for womenfolk. I've a cousin like that,' Jared added. 'Although, he's grown up some since he adopted a little girl. Becoming a father has changed his view about women.'

Abruptly, the door to the apartment was flung open!

Jared spun about − his gun leapt into his hand. A man who had started into the apartment hit his brakes, nearly falling down from skidding on his heels.

'Whoa!' he cried, throwing his hands in the air. 'Don't shoot!'

'Mitch!' Crystal cried. 'What on earth. . . ?'

Jared glared at the man. 'Were you raised by wild dogs, friend?' he snapped. 'No man ought to enter a single lady's dwelling without knocking first.'

Mitch was average in size and build, with rusty-brown colored hair and dusky brown eyes. He was wearing a gun, but the holster was wrapped almost behind his right hip as if the weapon was a secondhand thought. Mid-twenties, he was not a bad-looking sort . . . reminded Jared a little of Cliff, the cousin he had mentioned to Crystal.

'It's all right, Mr Valeron,' the lady hurried to explain. 'Mitch is a friend of mine. He's the one I sent the wire to, letting him know I was returning home.'

'I didn't mean to rush in like a mustang through a crack in the fence,' Mitch apologized to Jared. Then turning to the lady, 'It's just that someone said you were back. I've been worried to death about you. Did you find the man who killed your brother? I was. . . .' He stopped in mid-sentence and his eyes bugged in shock. 'Did you call this guy Valeron?'

Jared holstered his gun and took a seat on one of the stools. He waved a hand at the girl, as if to brush aside a pesky fly. 'You best explain to your lovelorn admirer how we came to be together. Wouldn't want him getting the wrong idea.'

'Mitch Winters!' Crystal spouted sternly. 'What's the idea of bursting into my apartment without knocking first? Mr Valeron might have shot you dead!'

He took on a hang-dog look, shoulders slumped and head lowered. 'I'm sorry, Crystal,' he murmured like a scolded child. 'I've been worried sick about you, wondering if. . . .' He waved a hand in a helpless gesture, 'I plumb forgot my manners.'

'Close the door and sit down,' Crystal invited, relaxing her rigid posture. 'I suppose you do deserve an explanation.'

Jared snickered to himself and muttered: 'This ought to be good.'

CHAPTER FIVE

It was late afternoon and Jared walked alongside Mitch down the main street of town.

'Now that we've had a meal and left the young lady to rest up,' Jared spoke up, 'how about you fill me in on this mining burg? A blacksmith-liveryman usually keeps tabs on the goings on about town, yet you never saw this guy from the drawing?'

'The Quick-Silver mine is a couple miles back in the hills, I spend a lot of time doing my blacksmith work up there. I've got myself a portable forge up at the mining site. I spend three days a week sharpening drill bits, fixing ore cars and mending things. My younger brother Toby handles things down here while I'm gone. He mostly runs the stable and oversees the horses and wagon rentals, so he leaves the harder jobs, like welding or building from scratch, till I'm available.'

'How long have you been courting Crystal?'

He groaned in defeat. 'I've been trying since the first day I saw her.' At Jared's glance, he clarified. 'I've some-times danced with her at the weekly social and sat next to her at the Sunday meeting one time. But she barely allows me to hold her hand, and we've yet to have any special time together, just the two of us.'

'Not much of a relationship for you to have lent her a horse and saddle.'

Mitch made a face. 'I had no choice. When Crystal sets her mind to something. . . . Well, I couldn't say no to her. I'd have went with her, but my brother can't handle the work up at the mine yet. There's no way I could leave, I'd have lost everything I've worked for these past three years.'

Jared reached into his pocket and removed a wad of bills. 'I got a hundred dollars for the horse and saddle you lost,' he explained. 'It's all the livery man in Castle Point was willing to pay. It was either that, or you would have had to make the trip over there and bring them back.'

'No. I appreciate the money,' Mitch thanked him, tucking the cash in his pocket. 'It's less than I would have gotten selling them myself, but there's no way I would have had the time to go and fetch them back.'

Jared got back to his questions. 'It there anyone else in Crystal's life?'

'A good many guys are chasing after her, but the main man in her life was her brother.' He explained the situation further. 'Donny was more than a big brother. After their folks died, he looked after Crystal and shared his place with her. The two of them moved here when Donny landed a bookkeeping job at the saloon.'

'A good bookkeeper ought to have stayed in Boulder. I saw the university. There must be dozens of jobs in that city for a man who's good with numbers.'

'That's where Adour's accountant came from. However, Crystal told me Donny wanted to get some

51

experience so he could be on his own and open his own office one day. He wanted to manage books for several companies.'

'One of my cousins is a combination attorney and accountant. He taught my sister the ins and outs of book-keeping. She learned enough to oversee several businesses in Valeron.'

'It's the only way to earn a decent living,' Mitch said. 'A regular bookkeeper makes about the same as a grocery clerk. Lariquett offered him twice the money he was earning in Boulder, so they moved into the apartment above the hardware store.'

'You said Adour has an accountant, too?'

'Yeah, a college-educated fellow, name of Frye. I've heard he has several years' experience and also oversaw Donny's books. I recall Crystal telling me that Jacques Adour made Frye a great offer and turned all of the accounting to him.'

'And this Lariquett, he's an alley cat sort around women?' Jared recalled Crystal had said Donny warned her to stay away from the saloon owner. 'What else can you tell me about the two men who run this town?'

'Jacques's folks were Creole French. He used their wealth to make his own fortune. His pretty wife, Sylvia, is quite a bit younger than him. Jacques and her make business trips to Boulder to visit the theater and for shopping. It's no secret his wife also goes to Denver several times a year for the same reason.'

'And does Jacques always go with her?'

'Jacques's elderly spinster sister accompanies her, kind of like a chaperon. The woman also earns her keep doing housework and preparing meals. On occasion, the two of them are escorted by one of his hired men. As for the marriage, they seem happy together.'

'A beautiful woman . . . sounds as if the lady would be a prime target for Lariquett.'

'Only if he wanted to end up broke and out on his rump.'

'I thought he owned the saloon?'

'It's true the two of them started this town together, but Jacques is the man who financed it all. Lariquett had a saloon that burned down and left him broke. Jacques brought him along when he acquired a small mine, which he named Quick-Silver. When they struck a rich ore, he used his personal wealth to develop the digging. Jacques loves the idea of having his own mining operation. He financed the saloon and turned it over to Lariquett to manage. He also lets him oversee the rest of the town. On the surface, Lariquett has the power, but Donny once told me the man doesn't actually own anything. He gets to sit in the driver's seat, but Jacques owns the horse and wagon.'

'This town looks to be booming!'

Mitch bobbed his head. 'It is, and every dime goes to Jacques Adour. He pays Lariquett a good salary and a small percentage of the profit, along with funds for running the town. Fact remains, everyone in Quick-Silver is basically working for the Frenchman.'

'If Lariquett is more of a manager than an owner,' Jared wondered, 'Why would someone want to kill his bookkeeper?'

Mitch clicked his tongue in puzzlement. 'Donny was as honest as the sun and didn't drink or gamble. I can't imagine why anyone would want him dead.'

'According to Crystal, he was targeted. The man called him by name and pushed him into a fight. She said he threatened to kill him outright if he didn't go for his gun.'

Mitch said gravely, 'A lot of men up here wear a gun – even me, but I don't know that Donny had ever taken his out of its holster. He was a brainy sort, not the kind of man to get into any kind of fight.'

Jared rubbed his jaw thoughtfully. 'Why choose a book-keeper for a fight? Could he have discovered that someone was skimming cash or the like?'

'Donny only did the books for the saloon and casino,' Mitch advised him. 'Like I told you, old man Adour has Frye to oversee both the mine and every other business he owns. Crystal says Frye audited Donny's books weekly. If anyone noticed something amiss, it would have been Frye.'

The two of them had reached the livery and blacksmith. A youthful-looking fellow, showing the first whiskers of a mustache and resembling Mitch, came forward to greet them.

'This is Toby, my younger brother,' Mitch introduced. 'Tobe . . . this is Jared Valeron.'

Toby's jaw came unhinged. 'Valeron?!' His voice squeaked and his eyes opened wide.

Mitch waved a hand to dismiss whatever else his brother might have been about to say. 'The guy who killed Donny was not Wyatt Valeron; it was someone using his name.'

'Boy, howdy!' Toby exclaimed. 'Who in the world would be that stupid?'

Mitch dug his elbow into Jared's ribs. 'See? We done heard of the Valerons way up here in the hills.'

'Wyatt got around some,' Jared said. Then he stuck out his hand, 'Glad to meet you, Toby.'

The young man's grip was firm, and his arms – much the same as Mitch – showed the power from using hammers and tools that came with the blacksmith trade.

'Do you remember this guy?' Jared asked, showing Toby the drawing Sketcher had made.

Toby immediately replied, 'Yeah, I seen him. The man was about as sour as a green lemon. Come walking from the railroad station and asked if there was a hotel. I pointed out the only rooming house in town, and he wandered off without another word. He didn't stay but the one night at the hotel. Next thing, he has gunned down Donny Duval and hopped back on the train.'

Jared posited. 'He came to town with the single purpose of killing Donny.'

'Boy, howdy!' Mitch declared. 'That proves it was murder.'

'Tell you straight,' Toby jumped into the conversation, 'I was right shocked when people started saying the killer was Wyatt Valeron. We read about that deal a few months back, over at Solitary, Wyoming. Sounds like you Valerons were on the verge of a full-scale war.'

'Never had to fire a shot,' Jared shrugged off the conflict. 'After we blew their tool shed to bits, to prove we were serious, the guilty parties come along about as meek as scolded dogs.'

'The story in the newspaper sounded somewhat more exciting.'

'Can't believe anything you read in print these days. They write whatever they think will increase their sales.'

'Might have been a little extra smoke,' Mitch chipped in with a grin, 'but I'd wager there was some fire all the same.'

'Regardless, guys. I'm not figuring on calling in any help on this trip, not unless it turns out one of the big dogs of this burg is responsible for Donny being murdered. I promised Miss Duval we would find out who hired the phony gunman. Then I'll track down the killer. Both of those men are living on borrowed time, and I intend to darn well stop their clocks!'

Toby punched his brother's shoulder lightly. 'Now, that sounds more like the Valerons we've read about in the paper.'

The next day, Jared left the hotel, had breakfast, then met Mitch at the livery. Mitch had another day until he had to return to the mine, so he agreed to wander about and speak to some of the people, including anyone he encountered from the mine.

Jared, meanwhile, tackled the chore of interviewing the man who ruled Quick-Silver. He ventured over to a large, two-storey building on the main street of town, where Jacques Adour had his office. He had questions only Adour could answer, and he also wanted to talk to his accountant. Crystal had told him the top floor of the building housed the man's business office and a couple of other rooms. One was used by his wife. She supposedly liked to paint and also did sewing or reading to pass her time. The other was a private cubicle for the company accountant to do his bookkeeping.

The entrance had a big sign stating 'Adour Enterprises – Authorized Personnel Only'. Jared found the door was unlocked, so he entered the structure. A quick look around told him the bottom floor was used for storage, shipping and receiving. He took note of a holding area where there were boxes, crates and even a couple of pieces of furniture. One person was sitting at a desk, checking paperwork – likely comparing packing lists against payment vouchers or the like. He paid no attention to Jared, totally engrossed in his work.

Jared paused at the stairway, taking a moment to read a second sign. It stated that no one was allowed upstairs without an appointment. Jared ignored the warning and climbed the steps to the second floor. That's when he ran into a human roadblock.

The roadblock was a brute a couple of sizes bigger than a yearling bull, attired in a brown suit, and clean shaven except for a thick mustache. His looks showed a grain of intelligence, and he was planted in front of a closed door. It also had a painted notice that read 'Private'.

The brute placed his huge paws on his thick hips and glowered at Jared.

'You miss the signs out front and at the bottom of the stairs?' Brute asked, giving Jared an impudent once over.

Jared flashed an easy smile. 'The one that said no one could enter without permission – that sign?'

'That's the one.'

'Must have missed it,' Jared scoffed. 'I'm here to speak to Jacques Adour.'

'You need to make an appointment,' Brute insisted.

'This is personal, not business,' Jared explained.

'Don't make no difference,' Brute growled the words. 'No one sees Mr Adour without his say-so . . . and you haven't got it.'

Jared grinned. 'You remind me of my cousin. Ever hear of Lightning Rod Mason? He used to live in Denver.'

Brute frowned with recognition. 'I saw him fight at a

carnival one time. Tough cookie, your cousin.'

'He tried to teach me some of his moves, but I don't like to get physical,' he said, tapping the gun on his hip. 'Comes to trouble, I tend to let this Colt do my talking.'

'You're asking for trouble right now!' Brute asserted. 'Make an appointment or get lost!'

'I don't need an appointment, just a few words with your boss,' Jared persisted. 'I'd as soon not have to force my way in. It would make you look inept at your job.'

'What's that there word inept mean?'

'In-com-pe-tent,' Jared spoke the word one syllable at a time. 'Which means you are going to end up on the floor.'

Brute thrust his jaw forward and doubled his huge fists. 'You ain't Lightning Rod Mason,' he sneered. 'You get outta line with me and I'll bust you into firewood. So spin around and walk away . . . while you can still walk.'

'OK . . . OK!' Jared acquiesced, raising both hands with palms outward, as if signaling surrender . . .

As Brute relaxed his offensive posture, Jared did a swift kick and nailed him flush on the knee. The leg buckled from the sudden pain and Jared charged into the man, shoving against his chest with both hands. The fellow could not catch himself or keep his balance; he crashed into and through the door, landing flat on his back just inside a spacious office. A few feet away was a large, expensive-looking desk.

An elderly, nearly bald man sprang up from his chair, eyes wide and his mouth agape. His hands were on his desktop, while his alarmed gaze went from his guard on the floor to the man standing over him.

'Howdy!' Jared addressed him with a grin, now holding a gun on Brute. 'This fellow said you wouldn't speak to anyone without an appointment. I wonder if you'd make an exception this one time?'

The old boy sputtered pompously. 'What's the meaning of this? Who are you? And how dare you attack my security guard!'

'I'm not here to cause any trouble, Mr Adour. I just need a few minutes of your time.'

He sputtered pompously. 'And why should I give you a single minute of my time?'

'Because I'm a deputy US marshal,' Jared announced, taking liberties with the badge Brett had previously given him. 'And I'm asking . . . polite like.'

Sitting up, Brute snorted while rubbing his leg. 'Polite he says . . . after he about broke my knee!'

Jared pinned him with a hard look. 'If I'd have kicked you on the side of your knee, you'd have been crippled for a month. That little tap will wear off in a couple hours and you'll be back to your intimidating self in no time.'

'You could have made an appointment,' Jacques sniffed importantly. 'I don't have a lot of time for. . . .'

'For murder?' Jared interjected.

The statement stopped him cold. 'Murder?' his voice raised to a higher pitch. 'Whatever are you talking about?'

CHAPTER SIX

Now that Jared had Jacques Adour's full attention, he holstered his gun. 'I'm referring to the killing of Donny Duval,' Jared stated it as a fact. Walking around Brute, he stopped in front of Adour's desk.

'It's obvious as the nose on your face – Donny was intentionally braced and executed by a dirty, lowdown, fourth-rate gunhand.'

'Wyatt Valeron ain't no fourth-rate gunhand,' Brute tossed the words at Jared, still sitting on the floor.

'You couldn't be more right,' Jared agreed. 'But it wasn't Wyatt Valeron who shot and killed Donny Duval. Wyatt was a hundred miles away, starting a new life with his bride, when the shooting took place. I aim to find the craven, gutless gunnie who sullied his name.' Hedging his words with ice, he added: 'And I'll darn well track down and kill the yellow-bellied coward who hired him, too!'

'A deputy US marshal wouldn't do that,' Jacques stated. 'There are rules, laws in place that. . . .'

'This is personal, Mr Adour,' Jared fumed. 'It's a matter of honor, and I'm honor-bound to clear Cousin Wyatt's name!'

'Cousin Wyatt?' the old gent's brow crested. 'Then you are a Valeron, too?'

'Jared Valeron,' he introduced himself.

'What does any of this have to do with me?' Jacques asked, appearing a bit more subdued.

'I'd like to scratch you from my list of suspects.'

Brute managed to get on his feet. He looked at Jacques. 'You want me to get some help? I don't care what kind of badge he flashes, we can toss this guy out on his ear.'

'Go walk off the bruise to your knee, Lex,' Jacques ordered. 'I'll speak to the gentleman.'

Jared ignored the sarcastic tone and turned his head toward the guard. 'Too much confidence in your size leaves you open for an experienced fighter, Lex. Always keep your distance until you know the intent of your opponent and what he is capable of.'

The big man didn't reply, only grumbled a curse under his breath. Once he had closed the door − of which the latch was now broken − Jacques sat back down. He sighed with a grim resignation.

'Ask your questions, young man.'

Jared showed him the sketch, but he didn't recognize the man. Then he hit him with several queries, studying his answers for any signs of guilt or suspicion. It took less than two minutes to dismiss the ruler of Quick-Silver as a culprit.

'I regret barging in the way I did,' Jared made a peace offering. 'Every day it takes to learn who the impostor is allows him to get farther away and be harder to find.'

'Lex can fix the door,' Jacques was gracious. 'However, I would appreciate having you make an appointment next time. Simply speaking to the clerk downstairs would be enough to get word to me.'

'Again, I apologize.' Jared shrugged. 'Actually, I'm not known for my patience. Some even claim I have a hair-trigger temper.'

'Can't imagine how you got such a reputation,' Jacques replied dryly.

'Would you mind if I speak to your bookkeeper? I've heard he is a college man.'

'First in his class,' Jacques stated, back to demonstrating a superior air. 'I only hire the best.'

'It won't take me but a few minutes and I'll be out of your hair,' Jared assured him, immediately thinking that wasn't a very smart remark, considering Adour had very little hair left. Nonetheless, the man gave his nod of approval and pointed to the door leading to the rest of the upstairs apartment.

Entering the first adjoining room, Jared discovered it to be decorated with a large curtained window, and the walls were painted pink with yellow trim. There was an expensive-looking settee of a flowered design, three padded chairs and a couple of paintings on the wall. Sitting in front of an easel was a blonde woman. Her hair was held back with a bright pink ribbon, and she had wonderfully sculptured features, poised with a small brush in her hand. She paused to regard him with curious powder-blue eyes.

Jared stopped to admire her and she reciprocated his interest with a comely smile. The gesture added to the brightness of the room. In her mid- to late-twenties, she wore a paint-bespattered apron over an expensive-looking lavender gown to protect the material and white lace trim. More than pretty, she was breathtaking.

'You're Mrs Adour?' he asked, somewhat tongue-tied at being so close to such a lovely woman.

'I am,' she replied in a mellow, angelic tone of voice. 'And you are?'

Jared swept the hat from his head and bowed shortly. 'Jared Valeron, madam.'

'Charmed to meet you, Mr Valeron.'

Jared moved a couple steps to the side, able to see the canvas upon which she had been painting. He gave a nod of approval of her efforts. 'Very nice,' he said. 'And the pictures of mountains and flowers on the walls. . . .' he used his hat to point. 'Your handiwork?'

'Obviously, they are not of a professional level, but, yes, I painted them.'

'We've a fellow on our ranch – we call him Sketcher – and he's about the best artist I ever seen.'

Removing the drawing from the inside of his shirt, he showed it to the lady. 'This is a sketch of the man who shot Donny Duval. He drew it from Crystal Duval's memory.'

'Very lifelike,' the woman said, peering at the drawing. 'However, the face is not familiar to me.'

Jared put away the paper. 'Sketch doesn't do actual paintings. But these of yours are as good as the ones I've seen sold in stores.'

Another demure simper at his praise. 'You're very gracious.'

Jared turned to business. 'Did you personally know Donny Duval?'

A sadness entered her face. 'He came up to visit Mr Frye every Monday morning with the weekly casino reports. We didn't speak except in passing, but he seemed a most pleasant young man.'

'I'm looking into his murder,' Jared announced, watching for her reaction.

Her elegant brows lifted in surprise. 'Murder? I was told it was a gunfight.'

'Donny carried a gun, but Crystal said he only carried it because it was required . . . something about security for the saloon and casino.'

'Yes, all of the male employees working there tote a gun,' Mrs Adour confirmed.

'Crystal told me Donny never shot it much. He showed her how to shoot one time, but he never practiced with it.'

'Your point?' the lady wanted to know.

'She claimed the man who killed her brother gave him no choice. He called Donny by name, and he intended to shoot him whether he went for his gun or not. Donny was shot three times in the chest and never got his gun out of the holster.'

'Why would someone want to kill Donny?'

'His sister has no idea,' Jared replied. 'For myself, I believe Donny must have known or saw something he shouldn't. Someone wanted to silence him before he said anything, so they hired a killer to gun him down.'

A hint of – Fear? Concern? Guilt? – flashed in the woman's eyes, but her voice remained calm. 'That seems a rather wild assumption. Do you have special information to support such a conclusion?'

'The man who killed him used my cousin's name,' Jared explicated. 'Probably thought it would help with his cowardly deed and escape. No one in their right mind would want to question Wyatt Valeron about his motives. He has a reputation no sane man would challenge.'

'But it wasn't him who did the shooting.'

'No,' he acknowledged her statement. 'So I'm trying to discover the reason why the young fella was killed. It's the only way I know to track down this pretender.'

Mrs Adour lowered her gaze. 'Surely, you don't suspect my husband had anything to do with Donny's death?'

'He struck me as a little too proud a type of man to resort to disreputable violence. In his position as monarch over this entire town he need only wave his hand to be rid of anyone he wanted.'

'My husband does wield authoritative control over the lives of most everyone living in Quick-Silver,' the lady concurred.

Jared grinned. 'With him being the king, I reckon that makes you queen.'

She indulged his remark with grace. 'I spend much of my reign taking trips to Boulder or Denver. There may be some who consider me Jacques's queen, but I don't share his throne in this beyond-the-woods settlement. He lives to make money, while I prefer to spend it. I keep hoping he will retire so we can experience some of the finer things we can afford before he is too old to enjoy it.'

'At his age, he might not be able to keep up with . . . all of a younger lady's needs,' Jared suggested, at the risk of incurring her wrath. 'Could be, he'll live longer working up here.'

Surprisingly, she laughed at his candid statement. 'Perhaps you're right, Mr Valeron. He is almost twenty years older than me and doesn't take as good of care of himself as he should.'

Jared breathed a sigh of relief that she hadn't taken offense. 'It's been the high point of my week meeting you, Mrs Adour. I'll take my leave from your charming company as I need to have a few words with your husband's accountant.'

'It's been diverting meeting you too, Mr Valeron. Just tap lightly on the door and enter. Mr Frye is always available for visitors.' She laughed softly. 'Being locked away like he is, an interruption to his tedious job is usually appreciated.'

Jared kept his hat in his hand as he walked over and did as she had instructed. So far, he had nothing to go on. Perhaps a chat with the accountant would give him a clue or starting place.

Upon his return to the Duval apartment, Jared found Crystal pacing the floor. She was obviously on edge, forced to remain behind while he and Mitch did the investigating.

'So?' She could not restrain her anxiety. 'What did you learn? Who did you talk to? Do you know why Donny was killed? Do you have any idea who is behind his murder?'

Jared raised his hands to calm her. 'Rein in your steed, little lady. This is not a sprint to the finish line. We have to take small steps and uncover one clue at a time.'

She balled her small fists at her sides. 'But you must have an idea or two by now!'

'Mitch and I have started the boulder rolling downhill. We'll know something by the time it hits the bottom. You have my word on that.'

'Steeds, boulders . . . I need answers and you give me inane metaphors!'

'Dad gum, you have read a lot of books – inane metaphors? My aunt Faye is the best-educated woman on our ranch, but I've never heard anyone talk better than you. How come you're not a school teacher?'

'I don't have the required patience!' she snapped.

The young lady strode around the room again before stopping in front of Jared. He could see the frustration, worry and anger in the glow of her ebony eyes and the tightness of her jaw. Even fired up and flustered, she forced a calm into her voice.

'It's just that. . . .' she pressed her lips into a thin line. 'I'm going crazy! I can't sleep, I can't eat, I can't even think straight. There must be something I can do to help.'

'You got me a sketch of Donny's killer, Miss Duval,' he attempted to placate her host of turbulent emotions. 'That will lead me to him, but whoever is behind the death of your brother might be willing to kill again. I'm not going to risk your life.'

'I should have some say about what risks I can take.'

Jared maintained a steadfast resolve. 'I promised you I would get the man responsible . . . and I will. I know it's hard, but you have to find the patience to let me do the job. One mistake, we push too fast and get careless, and the person behind Donny's killer might spook. If that happens, it will make the job a lot tougher, and more dangerous too.'

She fixed him with an intensive stare that would have caused a grizzly to back down. After a long peruse, she exhaled a breath and allowed her shoulders to sag. 'I want to trust in you,' she murmured, the emotion blocking her words. She lifted her hands in a helpless gesture and took a step closer. 'It's just so . . . so very hard. And the pain of losing Donny is. . . .' Her voice cracked with a sob.

Jared reached out in a consoling gesture. However, Crystal's need for comfort went beyond hand-holding. She came into his arms, buried her face against his chest . . . and began to weep. This wasn't a sniffle or controlled cry, the sobbing racked her until her entire body shook.

Taken aback, Jared clumsily held her close, allowing her to release the heartache and suffering she had been keeping inside. Crystal had likely needed a good cry ever since her brother's death. Obviously, her strength and resolve had caved under the weight of everything that had happened.

After sustaining the embrace for some time, the weeping ceased. Jared produced a hankie for her and guided the girl over to the bed. He sat down at her side as she removed the moisture from her cheeks. He kept his arm around her and she leaned back to rest her head against his shoulder.

'You must think I'm little more than a child,' she murmured after a time.

'Hardly that,' Jared told her firmly. 'A person can't carry around a world of hurt forever – it would destroy them. Crying is a gift from Heaven, a way of easing the pain. Everyone needs a good cry now and again.'

'I doubt you've ever cried.'

'I'm not made of stone,' he admitted. 'I cried when I was a young man after learning that a favorite cousin of mine had been killed by a band of Indians. And I shed a few tears back when my favorite horse died. Like I said, it's the Lord's way of allowing us to deal with the pain of a tragic loss.'

Crystal straightened to sit upright and gazed at him. He was immediately struck by her tantalizing expression. She had been keeping her guard up ever since she took a shot at him. This time, she appeared vulnerable . . . gentle . . .

beautiful. There was something more in her expression, peaceful, soft, inviting. . . .

'I visited Mrs Adour this morning,' he related honestly. 'While she is a stunning woman, she pales beside you for pure, genuine beauty.'

Crystal's lips parted, as a slight flush crept into her cheeks. 'I . . . I can't believe you mean that.'

Jared smiled. 'I'm not much at flattery, little lady. I can only speak from my heart.'

Oddly, the girl dreamily closed her eyes and slightly pursed her lips.

Surrendering to a yearning from deep inside, he turned towards her and kissed her ever so gently. Surprisingly, she returned the kiss, warm . . . wonderful. . . .

Then, abruptly, Crystal broke contact! Her eyes blinked open wide, a shocked look flooded her features . . . and she slapped Jared's cheek with an open palm!

Although the degree of force was minor, he recoiled instantly from her action – at the exact moment the door opened!

'What's going on?' Mitch growled angrily. 'Jared! What the hell?

Jared jumped to his feet, though he put his attention on Crystal. 'I'm sorry, Miss Duval, I. . . .' but he had no words at his command.

She too sprang to her feet. 'No!' she uttered softly. 'I'm sorry for. . . .' But she couldn't continue either.

'What about me?' Mitch whined. 'Should I be sorry? Angry? Should I apologize for entering the room without knocking?'

'It's a habit you ought to consider, Mitch!' Jared

quipped. 'I might have killed you.' Thinking on it a moment, he declared: 'I still might!'

'Yeah? If you hadn't been so busy doing. . . .' he scowled. 'Just what were you doing?'

Jared recovered his wits and laughed. 'It's not what it looked like. It was—'

'None of your business, Mitch Winters!' Crystal snapped angrily, shutting down Jared's lame alibi. 'I told you the last time not to come storming through my door without knocking first!'

Mitch cowed from her harsh dressing down. 'I didn't . . . I mean, I knew Jared was here. I. . . .'

'Forget it,' Jared let him off the hook. Then putting his attention back on the girl, he displayed a beg-your-pardon expression.

'I don't know what happened to my self-control, Miss Duval. I didn't mean to ruin a caring and comforting moment.'

Thankfully, Crystal laughed. 'I acted without thinking as well. How about we forget our single lapse of common sense?'

'That would suit me fine – it never happened.'

Mitch scratched his head and asked, 'So what did happen?'

Jared and Crystal's eyes met briefly and they replied in unison: 'Nothing happened.'

An important part of Rizzo's job was to be Lariquett's eyes and ears around town. He did most of the dirty work when it was required, keeping out drifters, troublemakers and union organizers. He had been the one who suggested and located the gunman, a man he simply called Sutter, to kill Donny Duval.

'We've some trouble brewing,' Rizzo informed Lariquett, after finding him at his office on the second floor of the casino. 'That character who arrived with Crystal is asking a lot of questions.'

'And?'

'It's one of them queer stories a person can't hardly believe, Chief.' Rizzo's lips curled in a cocky smirk. 'Wormed it out of Toby Winters while he was shoeing my horse. Mitch and the stranger appear to have teamed up together. I wasn't sure what it was all about, so I talked to Toby.'

'Yes, yes,' Lariquett showed his impatience. 'Get on with the story. What about the girl and this new man about town?'

'Crystal is more than a fine-looking filly,' he praised. 'Toby said the gal actually tried to kill a Valeron.'

'Damn!' Lariquett was shocked. 'I'd never have given her credit for that kind of courage.'

'Yep,' Rizzo said with a smirk. 'She missed the guy, but he returned fire and put a slug through her shoulder!'

'What?' Lariquett yelped. 'A Valeron shot Crystal?' He harrumphed at the news. 'So who's the fella who came back to town with her?'

'That's the real joker in the deck, Chief,' Rizzo finally gave him the critical information. 'He's the man she shot at – none other than Wyatt Valeron's cousin.'

Lariquett felt an immediate churning within his stomach. 'A Valeron!' he gasped. 'How on earth did. . . ?'

Rizzo stopped his question, explaining the details about how Valeron had shot Crystal, not knowing she was a woman. He grunted when he'd finished. 'Can't imagine any decent woman dressing up like a man. And Crystal sure don't seem the sort to disgrace herself that way.'

'Donny and her were very close. We knew she had left on a vendetta, but I figured she would get the law involved or hire a gunman to help her.'

'It's worse than that, Chief.'

'Nothing leads back to us,' Lariquett said with confidence. 'Valeron won't find a thing.'

Rizzo skewed up his face into a doubting pucker.

'What?' Lariquett demanded, seeing he had been holding something back.

'They have a drawing of Sutter.'

Lariquett threw his hands in the air. 'How is that possible?'

'No idea, but me and the boys have kept eyes on Valeron since he showed up. Toby said the sketch was as good as a photograph – he recognized Sutter right off. A'course he don't know his name, but this might spell trouble.'

'Damn it all, Rizzo! This is getting out of hand!'

The man snorted his own concern. 'It don't get no better, Chief,' he admitted. Then he related how Valeron and Mitch were questioning people both at the mine and all over town. Lastly, he hit him between the eyes with the hard news.

'Valeron visited Adour this morning, too.' He chuckled. 'Made a complete fool out of the old man's buffoon watchdog, Lex. Seen him hobbling around when he went to lunch. Seems Valeron kicked him on the knee and forced his way in to talk to Adour.'

'So what? Jacques doesn't know squat and couldn't care less.'

Rizzo continued to display a skeptical look. 'I don't know if this is related to Valeron's visit, but Mrs Adour and her spinster sister-in-law packed a couple of bags and took the afternoon train for Boulder.'

'That woman goes shopping more often than some people visit an outhouse. Why should that strike you odd?'

'It's the timing of the trip,' Rizzo said. 'I gotta wonder if Valeron said or did something when he talked with Jacques. Could be he prompted their trip to either Boulder or Denver.'

'You are getting to be a real worrier, Rizzo,' Lariquett chided him. 'You said yourself, no one in this town knows anything about the man who killed Donny.'

'It's true. I hired the man cause I had worked a few jobs way back when. He's the kind of man who can get falling-down drunk and still never shoot off his mouth. We rode together for nearly three years, right up to when he ended up in prison for six months.' He guffawed, 'All the jobs we pulled and he gets snagged for one stupid hold-up at a trading post.'

'You said he didn't snitch on you.'

'That's what I'm saying, Chief. We did the job together, but some law dog caught him at our camp while I was off fishing.' He sighed, 'Nope. Judge offered him a shorter sentence if he would give me up. Sutter didn't even blink. He did the six months.'

'Not much jail time for a hold-up,' Lariquett remarked.

'We didn't use no guns,' Rizzo told him. 'It was kind of a grab and run thing, due to us being too broke to buy anything . . . and we didn't want to hurt anyone. I mean Sutter held the man down while I collected what money he had stashed. We took a handful of chewing tobacco and a couple boxes of bullets – not much of a robbery. The man only had twenty dollars and some change.'

'So you hired on with me while he was in jail,' Lariquett deduced.

'Yeah, I was ready for an actual job. Pickings were mighty lean doing a robbery here or there. I figured a payday every month beat the heck out of starving and living on the run.'

'But not Sutter.' It was a statement.

'You give him his biggest payday since I've known him. I 'spect he's living the good life on Market Street, over in Denver, these days.'

'Until he runs out of money.'

'Keep me posted on Valeron's movements,' Lariquett ordered. 'Might ought to have one of the boys watch Mitch's movements, too. Everyone knows he has a fire burning for Crystal.'

'You got it,' Rizzo said. 'If they learn anything at all, we'll know about it.'

CHAPTER SEVEN

Brett Valeron arrived as his father was about to leave the house. Locke smiled, but didn't offer a verbal greeting. Brett didn't often visit without a special invite, having duties in town and a wife and baby to look after. If he had made the trip out, he had a purpose.

'How's it going, Pa?' Brett asked, stepping down from his horse. 'Don't suppose Shane is close by?'

'Hello to you too, son,' he responded. 'And, you're in luck. Shane is at the barn tending to a new foal. The mare got into some wild onion or something and the colt wouldn't take her milk. He and Mikki are supervising Nessy – she's playing the little mother.'

'I'd like to take a look at that,' Brett said, smiling at the news.

'Let's go,' Locke replied with some enthusiasm. 'They only got the milk ready a few minutes ago. The foal will likely need three or four to fill him up.'

The two of them hurried their step. Anyone who had ever bottle-fed a baby animal – be it lambs, calves or horses – knew it was great fun to watch. They entered the barn as Nessy was taking away an empty bottle and reaching for another.

'Wow!' the child cried gleefully. 'Bunny Boy is really thirsty!'

Locke frowned at Mikki. 'Since when would we ever name a horse Bunny Boy?'

Mikki, Nessy's nanny, laughed. 'You can guess who named him.'

'I swear,' Locke muttered good-naturedly, 'that child is running this entire ranch!'

Shane turned the bottle feeding over to Nessy and her nanny to step over and take his cousin's hand in a firm shake.

'Been a spell, Brett,' he said, as the colt eagerly went after the new bottle of milk. When it was nearly emptied, he asked, 'What brings you out to the ranch?'

Brett heaved a sigh. 'It's not a what . . . it's a who.'

'Jared!' Locke declared, not hiding his exasperation. 'What's your brother got himself mixed up in now?'

Rather than speak in front of the girls, Brett led the two of them out of the barn. He stopped once they were out of earshot.

'I got a telegraph message yesterday. Jared is at a mining town over in Colorado. He warned me that he was going to use the deputy US marshal's badge I gave him for emergency use and wanted me to vouch for him if needed.'

'This must have something to do with the wire asking Sketcher to come to Castle Point a week or so back,' Shane guessed. 'He's looking into whoever used Wyatt's name when they killed a girl's brother.'

Locke grew serious. 'If he's asked for your support, he must be having some trouble locating the phony gunman.'

'It could be more than one man,' Shane offered. 'I

spoke to Sketcher and he said the girl, who tried to shoot Jer, claimed there was no reason for the murder. Her brother did nothing but handle the bookkeeping for one of the businesses. He didn't have any enemies.'

'It's the reason I'm here,' Brett told the pair. 'I think Jerry might be in over his head. All he has to go on is the girl's word about the killing. Her brother might have been up to something and kept it from her. If Jerry gets tangled up in some kind of scheme, there might be several men to deal with. Plus, anyone who will gun down a bookkeeper on the main street of town wouldn't hesitate to back-shoot anyone investigating the murder.'

'You came to ask for help,' Shane concluded. 'Tell me where this place is and I'll get my gear.'

'Easy, Shane,' Locke cautioned. 'You're no gun hand.'

'Cliff is pretty good,' Brett volunteered, 'and he's been crying that we never let him lend a hand in these matters.'

Locke frowned. 'He has a daughter to look after.'

Shane chipped in, 'He is the best man with a gun here on the ranch. Doggie was a fair shot, but he quit to become a sheriff. As for Troy and Faro, Wendy could beat either of them at shooting.'

Brett laughed. 'And you know she would go to brother Jared's aid in one second flat. But she and July are going to slip into double-harness pretty soon. This isn't a chore for a girl about to wed.'

'I wouldn't take a chance sending her to a mining camp,' Locke said firmly. 'Look at how close she came to a real gunfight in Denver . . . and she was a pretend book-keeper!'

'I'll take Cliff,' Shane declared. 'If we should need more help, we'll send for it.'

Locke gave a nod of approval. 'Fine. Brett, you give directions to Shane as to how to find that mining town. Then you can head for home. Shane, soon as you know where you're heading, go round up Cliff. He's with a couple of men over in South Canyon mending the fence to our winter feed.'

Three days had passed and Jared and Mitch had found out almost nothing. Hardly anyone admitted having seen the shooter, and the people interviewed were less than sociable. Even Toby, who remembered seeing the guy, had learned nothing about him. The hotel had the gunman on their register as Wyatt Valeron, but had not listed any home town, territory or state.

Mitch was forced to cease his search and spend time at the mine. He had fallen behind in his work and took Toby with him. Jared volunteered to keep an eye on the stable and barn while he was gone. It meant he was stuck tending stock and renting horses or doing livery work. To break up the monotony the second day, Jared walked down to watch the arrival of the narrow-gauge train.

A couple men exited, then he saw Mrs Adour and her female companion get off. A big fellow who had been waiting for them walked up to get their luggage. Jared recognized it was the brute he'd humiliated at Jacques Adour's office. The two ladies did not wait for Lex, starting to walk in the direction of their house. Sylvia spotted him and lifted a hand in a short wave.

Jared smiled back and touched the brim of his hat, before heading back to the stable.

To his surprise, Mitch had returned and was checking to see that everything was copacetic at the livery.

'It's about time for lunch,' Mitch told Jared, displaying a sly grin. 'I made a point of being here today so I could take Crystal to dinner.'

'Would this be an actual date?'

'Close as I've ever got,' Mitch said. Then with a hard stare. 'It's not like I ever held her in my arms like you did!'

'We explained that to you. She was overcome by grief and I happened to be there. If you had been the one there to comfort her at the time, you would have been consoling her the same way.'

'I saw the kiss!' Mitch objected. 'The two of you were . . . were. . . .'

'That was my fault, a silly impulse. Did you miss the part where she slapped my face?'

'It wasn't much of a slap,' he charged. 'Didn't even leave a red mark.'

'Dang, but you can be a hard-headed dolt, Mitch,' Jared complained. 'I step aside, I tell you to muster the grit to give the girl your best effort, and you still yap at me like I stepped on your tail.'

'So what about this meal I've been planning?' Mitch wanted to know. 'You're not going to end up sitting between us are you?'

'Trust me, I'll stay out of your way.' Jared tapped his chest with a pointed finger. 'Just get in there, display a little confidence, and let Crystal know that you want to be more than friends.'

'OK, OK,' Mitch gulped to muster his courage. 'I'm going to her apartment and we'll head over to eat at the restaurant.'

'I'll stay out of your way,' Jared promised.

The man took a deep breath. 'Wish me luck,' he said

and hurried away to meet up with Crystal.

Jared also sighed, watching him go. If he was the type to settle down, he'd give Mitch some genuine competition. But a husband? A father? He shook his head and sauntered over to the barber shop. He would get a shave and a haircut. That would allow Mitch time to have a quiet meal alone with his gal.

As luck would have it, there was no waiting at the barber shop. He was sitting in the chair, being lathered up for a shave as Mitch and Crystal walked past. It caused a bit of a pang to sit there and do nothing. He had held the girl in his arms, kissed her sweet lips, and it felt very much like heaven. It nagged at him again as to whether he could ever give up the extended hunting trips and become a regular husband? Would tending the herd of horses with Shane be so bad?

He was lost in reverie for the next ten minutes, having an internal discourse about the pros and cons of marriage. Thankfully, that came to a sudden end as the barber removed the protective apron.

'Four bits, Mr Valeron,' the man proclaimed the price.

Jared handed him a dollar, picked up his hat, and walked out into the sunshine. He would have to wait a few minutes or find another eatery. He didn't intend to get in Mitch's way. Being caught with Crystal in his arms was bad enough. To show up while they were. . . .

'Mr Valeron?' a warm-melodic voice invaded his personal thoughts. He turned his head and was both shocked and pleased to see Mrs Adour had addressed him.

Removing his hat, he tipped his head in salutation. 'Didn't think you ever walked the streets by yourself, Mrs Adour,' was his greeting.

'Coleen is inside the restaurant arranging a table for our lunch. My husband takes most of his meals at his desk, so it's just my sister-in-law and me. I'd be pleased if you would dine with us.'

'Really?' He did not hide his surprise at the offer. 'Well, sure thing. I'd be proud as a peacock to join you . . . so long as it won't damage your reputation at being seen with me.'

She emitted a charming laugh. 'You should be aware, Mr Valeron – no one questions the King's royal mate.'

Jared chuckled at her wit.

Taking a step closer, she lowered her voice to little more than a whisper. 'I believe I have some information that might aid your investigation.'

He kept his own voice quiet so as not to be overheard by anyone near or passing by. 'Any help you can offer would be most welcome, Mrs Adour. I've been butting my head against a pretty hard wall.'

Reversing his direction to walk at her side, Sylvia's companion appeared at the door to the eating house. Jared felt a trace of heat flush his face and placed his hat back in place. He wondered what Mitch and Crystal would think seeing him enter the establishment with the queen of Quick-Silver.

Pausing at the entrance way, Sylvia introduced Coleen to Jared. He responded with a salutary nod, and proceeded with them, while making certain to catch Mitch's eye. As the trio approached a table in the back corner of the room, he winked at the blacksmith. Mitch showed surprise and quickly whispered something to Crystal, who turned her head to stare.

Ignoring her puzzled frown, Jared moved over and

pulled back a chair for Sylvia. He repeated the process for Coleen, then hung his hat on a nearby rack and took a seat facing Mrs Adour.

Sylvia waited until they had ordered their meal before she rested her forearms on the table and inched forward to speak privately to Jared.

'I took the liberty of visiting a friend of yours in Denver,' she began quietly.

'My friend?'

'A police sergeant named Fielding?'

Jared didn't hide his amazement. 'You spoke to Sergeant Fielding . . . about me?'

Sylvia scrutinized him. 'I wanted to know a little more about you. All I knew was what I have seen mentioned in a story or two in the Denver newspaper − we have a copy brought up on the daily train.'

'Can I ask why you were interested in me?'

Another reflective pause. 'I wanted to know if you were a man I could trust.'

'O-K,' he drawled, trying to determine what the statement meant.

'Gerald − Mr Frye,' she corrected, using their accountant's surname, 'He told me you had asked to see the weekly reports from the casino.' With a sly simper, she added: 'He also mentioned he very much doubted you had any real idea as to what you were looking for in the list of figures.'

'He plugged the target dead center,' Jared admitted, still in the dark about where this conversation was headed. 'I asked him if anything unusual had happened in the days before Donny was killed. I wondered if there might be a clue in the reports Crystal's brother turned in each week.'

'As it turns out, Mr Frye has previously noticed and reported several oddities to my husband.' Then she explained how the casino records included every gambling table and the winnings or losses from each employee. The records were used to keep track of how much each dealer earned for the house.

'The day before Donny died,' she elaborated, 'the casino figures showed two employees had very poor nights. Each dealer lost close to five hundred dollars.' She took a moment, allowing him to draw his own conclusion from that information, before continuing.

'My husband is aware that Andrew Lariquett skims a little extra cash from the casino each week. He pretty much ignores it, as long as it doesn't get out of hand. Andrew has always felt he should be better compensated for running the business. When looking over the past year, the two dealers who lost big are the same ones who lose on a regular schedule. The amounts are not excessive – usually each of them will lose a couple hundred dollars one night a week – but never on the same night.'

'So the thousand they lost between them could have been a payment of some kind,' Jared reasoned.

'Mr Frye stated it was the first time since he started keeping records that both dealers had lost so much on one single night.'

'How about their average winnings during the month? How do they compare with the others?'

'They always earn the least,' Sylvia said, her expression showing her conclusion. 'All of the dealers earn a percentage of their winnings. Mr Frye believes these two take a higher percentage than the others. It's likely they earn more so they will lose a set amount when instructed.'

'Makes sense. Lariquett would have to pay them more to buy their cooperation and silence.'

'It could be more than that,' Sylvia suggested. 'I believe the woman dealer has a . . . rather sordid past.' Jared lifted an eyebrow, and she added: 'Jacques told me Mr Lariquett once mentioned there was a handbill out for her arrest.' She removed a folded sheet of paper from her handbag. 'Sergeant Fielding provided this for me.'

Jared took the paper, scanned it quickly, then tucked it into his shirt. 'It could be the gal cooperates out of fear of being exposed.'

'That's my thinking as well.'

'Has your husband ever brought up the missing funds subject with Lariquett?'

'So long as it doesn't affect the overall earnings, Jacques isn't overly concerned. If the amounts become excessive or begin to hurt the total profit, then he will step in.' She lifted a slender shoulder in a shrug. 'As Mr Lariquett runs the casino and handles security for the entire town, my husband doesn't object to a few extra expenditures.'

The food was served, ending their discussion. Jared played the role of a gentleman, conversing about his sisters and family. It took all of his patience to sit there until Mrs Adour was finished and ready to leave. Then he quickly held the chair for Coleen and then Sylvia herself. He said farewell, but didn't escort the ladies to the door.

The bill was not a problem as Sylvia never paid for anything in the town of Quick-Silver. He had been their guest, so his meal was also included. He did think to drop a silver dollar on the table for the excellent service, before retrieving his hat. Rather than put it on, he carried it with him as he made his way over to Martin and Crystal. Both had long since finished their meal, but were sipping coffee, waiting for him to join them.

'You've stepped up to very elite company,' was Crystal's opening remark, as he pulled up a chair and dropped his hat on the table. 'I don't believe I've ever seen Mrs Adour and Coleen dine with anyone other than her husband.'

'I've an endearing personality – hadn't you noticed?'

'Um, let me guess the conversation,' Crystal quipped. 'You instructed her on how to skin a deer, or prepare a hide for making moccasins or gloves.'

Jared grinned at the ribbing. 'Actually, we talked mostly about accounting and bookkeeping. And, I might add, sharing a meal with them is going to pay some big . . . what's the word? – dividends.'

'Spill,' Mitch spoke anxiously. 'What did you learn?'

CHAPTER EIGHT

Rizzo stood in front of Lariquett's desk and gave his report.

'So nothing really stands out; Valeron hasn't learned anything.'

'There is one curious thing, Chief. Keogh and Blade told me they saw Mrs Adour stop Valeron on the street when she and Jacques' spinster sister were headed for the restaurant. Next thing, the man is sitting down with the two of them for a meal.'

The news brought Lariquett to his feet, a scowl darkening his face. 'What could Sylvia have been thinking, consorting with a known gunman?'

'Keogh watched them for a bit, but there's no way he could get close enough to hear anything. He did say Sylvia and Valeron seemed on the best of terms.'

Lariquett rubbed the stubble along his jawline. He hadn't made it to the barber yet today, but, presently, that was the least of his worries.

'Valeron teaming up with Sylvia is not a good combination,' he said. 'That man is beginning to annoy me.'

'You think Mrs Adour knows something that can hurt us?'

'It's hard to say,' Lariquett admitted. 'She is not a stupid woman. She might believe, because this guy is a Valeron, he is untouchable.'

'Don't make much difference, Chief. Ain't no way she can know about Sutter.'

'No, but there's an outside chance she suspects why Donny had to be eliminated.'

'One thing more,' Rizzo continued his report. 'Valeron sent a letter with the post going to Boulder. I seen him drop it off to be in the mail.'

'Could have been something to his folks or girlfriend. Who knows?'

'Leon recalled seeing the address when he stuck it in the sack – it was to the Boulder police.'

Lariquett frowned at the news. 'The Boulder police? What can that be about?'

'No idea, Chief. Maybe he is looking for information about Sutter.'

'Valeron is beginning to annoy me.'

'Perhaps it's time that me and the boys arranged an accident for him.'

He grunted. 'It would have to be done without anyone pointing a finger in our direction.'

'Do you have something in mind?'

'Valeron has made a lot of enemies over the last few years. Might even be someone around who would like to see him dead.'

'Who are we talking about?'

'Can't be one of our regular people. This calls for the services of someone special. Is Valeron staying at the hotel?'

'He is.'

Lariquett's eyes grew stone cold. 'Here's what I want you to do.'

A loud pounding on the door caused Crystal's eyes to pop open. Her heart leapt upwards in her throat as she scrambled out of bed and rushed to see what was the matter.

'Who is it? What do you. . . ?'

'Crystal! Open up! It's Mitch!'

She pulled the bolt to the side and opened the door. 'My goodness, Mitch!' she cried. 'What's happened?'

The man's chest was heaving, obviously having run for some distance. 'It's bad,' he gasped between breaths. 'I heard the shots – I was workin' late at the forge—' another gulp of breath. 'By the time I got to the hotel, a couple of men were shouting a man had been killed!' He paused to swallow enough air so he could speak again. Crystal's impatience consumed her. She grabbed him by the front of his shirt, tightly gripping the material in her hands.

'Tell me!' she wailed. 'It's not Jared?'

Mitch's head revolved back and forth. 'I don't know!' he gasped. 'The clerk said a man had busted into a room upstairs and all hell broke loose. That's all. . . .'

Crystal spun away, snatched up a robe and raced out of her apartment. Mitch didn't try to stop her, simply tried to keep up. He called after her: 'You don't even have your shoes on!'

But Crystal ignored him. Her eyes were filled with tears, and her heart pounded so hard it was like thunderclaps in her skull. She flew down the stairs and hit the street running. Mitch had trouble even keeping pace.

It can't be! Crystal's mind screamed. I can't be responsible for getting Jared killed!

There were a number of men standing about, everyone asking questions that no one could answer. Crystal pushed through the crowd and entered the hotel. Keogh and Blade were at the foot of the stairs, keeping any and all curious spectators at bay.

'Out of my way!' Crystal hissed, not slowing her steps.

'It ain't pretty,' Rizzo called from the top of the stairs. 'You don't need to see this, Miss Duval.'

Crystal shouldered her way between Rizzo's two goons and continued her ascent, not slowing until she reached Lariquett's number one man. Her look of determination caused him to hold his hands up, palms outward in a protective stance. He quickly moved aside to let her go by.

A few steps down the dim-lit hallway, she spied a man sitting on the floor, his chin resting on his chest. She was shocked to see a blood smear on the wall behind him, where he had obviously backed up against the partition and slid down to such a position after being shot.

Crystal rushed to Jared's room and stopped just inside the doorway.

The lamp had been turned up enough she could see the quilt on the bed had two large, ragged holes from shotgun blasts. However, the man standing in the corner was Jared!

Unconcerned with propriety, she charged into his arms, hugged him tightly, and clung to him.

'I thought it was you!' she managed through the constriction in her throat. 'When they said a man had been killed at the hotel. . . .'

'He came looking to do me mortal harm,' Jared told

89

her gently. 'Blasted my bed with two barrels of buckshot.'

She pushed back and stared at him. 'Then how. . . ?'

Jared nodded to his bedroll, which was on the floor next to the bed. 'I never trust a soft bed when I'm looking for a killer. Besides which, I'm used to sleeping on the ground.'

Looking at the pellet-riddled bunk, Crystal took a step back. 'What do you know that you haven't told me?' she wanted to know. 'Why would someone try to kill you?'

'Can't very well ask him now,' Jared sighed. 'Soon as I determined it wasn't another crazy gal shooting at me again by mistake I put two rounds squarely in the ambusher's chest. Do you have any idea who he is?'

Crystal turned away and moved over to take a closer look at the corpse. His eyes and mouth were open wide, the surprise of being killed frozen in his expression.

'I've never seen him before.'

Mitch, who had followed after Crystal quietly, inspected the dead man as well. 'He didn't leave his horse at the livery,' he made the observation. 'I'd have seen him. He must have come on the train.'

Rizzo moved closer with folded arms and glowered at Jared. 'You being a Valeron, I reckon you're the reason for this killer coming to our town. You're the one who ought to be able to identify him.'

Jared met the man's glare with a cold stare of his own. 'Actually, I would expect you to have the best idea as to who he is.'

'Yeah?' Rizzo jeered a challenge. 'Why is that?'

'Because you probably know who hired him.'

Jared's bluntness didn't faze the gunman. Instead, a smirk came into his face. 'You're a cocky sort, ain't you?'

'Not at all,' Jared replied. 'I've been told you oversee everything going on in this town. That being the case, you are more likely to know what this guy was up to than anyone else.'

Rizzo laughed dryly at the non-accusatory comeback. 'Regardless of the why or how, you are the victor tonight. We'll put this joker's body on display and see if anyone can identify your shooter.'

'I'd appreciate it . . . in case he has friends around.'

Crystal jumped into the verbal exchange. 'You darn well know why someone tried to kill Mr Valeron, Rizzo. It's because he is trying to find out why my brother was shot down in cold blood!'

The man shrugged, demonstrating no emotion. 'Far as I know, that was some drifter wanting to show off with a gun. He might have challenged anyone.'

'He sought out my brother,' she maintained stubbornly. 'He called Donny by name and said he was going to kill him. That is not the act of some drifter showing off with a gun!'

'I'm sorry about your brother, Miss Duval,' Rizzo said dispassionately. 'But he was wearing a gun. A bookkeeper ought to know better than pack iron on the streets of a lawless mining town. He made himself an easy target.'

Before Crystal could rebuke his statement, Jared nudged her over to Mitch. 'Take the lady home,' he told the blacksmith. 'It's late. And Miss Duval shouldn't be out in her night dress . . . especially without her shoes.'

Mitch laced his arm through the girl's. 'Come on, Miss Crystal,' he coaxed. 'There's nothing we can do here.' Then casting a glance at Jared. 'I've got a hay loft where you can bunk. Be a might safer than staying in this hotel.'

Jared waved his hand. 'I'll be fine. You two try to get some sleep.'

'Boy howdy!' Cliff exclaimed to Shane. 'Did you ever see so many beautiful girls?'

'Boulder has its share of husband hunters,' Shane replied. 'Fancy college, with lots of educated men. Bet most of those gals wouldn't give a couple of ranch-hand yahoos like us a second look.'

Cliff heaved an exaggerated sigh. 'Was a time, not so long ago, I'd jump in and round us up a couple of fine-looking fillies.'

'Mikki hasn't put her brand on you yet,' Shane referred to the nanny watching over Cliff's adopted daughter. 'You never had any qualms about chasing women before.'

'What do you think, Shane?' he asked seriously. 'Am I already sporting a wedding noose around my neck?'

'The belt buckle Nessy gave you for Christmas is bound to chase off a gal or two.'

'Oh, yeah,' Shane agreed. 'The word "Daddy" kind of advertises I'm in some kind of relationship.'

Shane scrutinized his cousin for a long moment. 'You might be able to use that to your advantage. Some girls might think you're looking for a wife and mother for your child, not a good time. There's nothing stopping you from sweet talking a couple of pretty girls for us.'

'Dad-gum, Shane!' he said, shaking his head woefully. 'I can't do it. I mean, the girls are there, prancing their wares and fluttering their lashes . . . yet I don't feel one tiny urge to hold any of them in my arms. What's the matter with me?'

'I've never had a full-blown case of it, so I can't say for

sure, but it sounds like the same infection Wyatt caught back when he got shot.'

Cliff displayed a forlorn expression. 'I knew it!' he declared. 'I felt it coming on from the first time I met Mikki. The fever, the sleepless nights, constantly pining about her. Durned if I haven't come down with a lethal dose of the love bug.'

'You've got all of the symptoms,' Shane agreed. 'Never thought a guy like you would catch a deadly disease like that.'

'It's your blasted side of the family,' he growled. 'You're the ones who are at fault!'

'What are you talking about, Cliff? How's it our fault?'

'Soon as I showed up, you Valerons started getting married!' He shook his fist. 'I knew the bunch of you were trouble, but I tossed my ante in with you. Next thing I know, I'm saddled with a seven-year-old little girl and Brett is taking the vows. I go to help my brother and he ends up married!

'Next thing, Nash ties the knot, then Reese . . . and Wyatt. . . .' he threw his hands in the air. 'Reese and Wyatt, for crying out loud!'

'Things just worked out, Cliff. Reese never figured to get married. Neither did Wyatt.'

'Even Sketcher has himself a wife and family!' Cliff cried. 'I mean, I didn't have a chance! You Valeron guys are a walking plague – the wedding disease! Every man on the place is in danger of catching it.' He groaned, 'And I sure enough got infected when Mikki arrived.'

Shane laughed at his dramatic delivery. 'Guess that leaves me and Jared as the only ones left, other than Faro and Troy.'

'No women at the mines or logging mill. I reckon them two are safe for the time being.'

Shane frowned, accepting the fact there would be no good times for them this night. 'The narrow-gauge train leaves early, unless you'd rather rent horses and ride up to Quick-Silver?'

'Let's head for our room,' Cliff grumbled. 'I hope I dream about Mikki . . . and it better be good! She owes me for giving me this bachelor-ruining condition.'

Shane chuckled. 'Who'd a'thunk: Cliff Mason, a romantic legend . . . brought down by love.'

Mitch joined Jared for breakfast but seemed in a dour mood. After cleaning his plate and having finished his coffee, Jared tried to pin him down.

'All right, Mitch,' he said. 'Enough of this silent brooding. What's stuck in your craw?'

'I can't help the way I feel, Jared, and I know it ain't your fault.'

'My fault? For what?'

Mitch lowered his head like he'd lost his best friend. 'For the way Crystal threw herself into your arms last night! I mean, there can't be no doubt she's got a fire burning for you.'

Jared didn't laugh, because the blacksmith was much too serious. Instead, he patted him on the shoulder. 'Cheer up, fella. You're reading the story from the wrong side.'

His eyes lifted cautiously. 'What're you talking about?'

'Crystal lost her brother,' Jared reasoned with him. 'Donny was her protector, the man who watched out for her.'

'Yeah? So what?'

'So, I have taken Donny's place.' Mitch frowned as he continued. 'Don't you see? I'm here to fulfill her vendetta, I'm the one with the gunfighting experience. She is looking to me to find Donny's killer. She doesn't see me so much as a suitor, but, rather, a temporary replacement for her brother.'

'That kiss sure. . . .'

Jared raised a hand to stop his argument. 'I keep telling you it was an impulsive thing, something neither of us planned. I admit, I had a weak moment. But you saw the end result − we both knew it was a mistake.'

He was unconvinced. 'She sure hugged you last night.'

'Yes . . . she hugged me . . . because I was still alive. She didn't try to kiss me, like a woman in love might have. It was a brotherly hug, not a heated embrace. See the difference?'

Mitch leaned back and studied Jared. He obviously wanted to believe what he was being told, but his jealousy had been primed. Accepting the argument, mulling it over in his head, he managed a degree of composure. He uttered a meaningless grunt and began to rub his hands together.

'You're saying Crystal thinks of you as a big brother,' he mused. 'You don't figure she's got a hankering for you.'

Jared acknowledged the statement. 'That's my take on our relationship, Mitch. I'm standing in for Donny, until we find his killer. Once the chore is finished, Crystal won't need me anymore.'

'I suppose you could be right,' he finally admitted. 'Like you said, she didn't kiss you last night. And a hug, well, that's something she would give to her big brother.'

'Now you're thinking straight. It's exactly as I keep telling you.'

Mitch perked up at the conclusion. 'Then I still have a chance.'

'Just don't give up on her,' Jared warned. 'The little gal has a host of emotions running wild since Donny's death, what with the grief and anger she's packing. Got to play this like a long-distance horse race. Don't run your steed too hard or he'll play out before the finish line. Pace yourself, test the competition, then ease into a front position and maintain your speed until you are standing at the winner's post . . . with Crystal at your side.'

'You have all the answers, Jared. I don't know if there's any meat to what you're saying, but I'll give Crystal my best effort.'

'And I'll give the same in finding out why Donny was killed.'

'What's your next move?'

'I'm going to use the information Mrs Adour provided.'

'This has gotten dangerous, Jared. Don't you think we need some special help, like a lawman of some kind?'

'I sent a letter to the law in Boulder telling them I was exercising my authority as a Deputy US Marshal. That should clear me for the shooting at my hotel room.'

'Carrying a badge won't stop a bullet in the back,' Mitch warned. 'You dodged those shotgun blasts by sleeping on the floor. The next time, the shooter might first make certain of his target.'

'I'll do the next part of my investigating on the sly. I know where those two dealers live.' He winked. 'And I'm sure they will be sleeping late due to working most of the night.'

'What can I do to help?'

'Keep an eye on Rizzo and his two clowns. If any trouble comes, it'll be from them.'

'Meaning you think Lariquett is behind Donny's murder.'

'He's top man up here, if you don't count Adour. After speaking to Jacques and his wife both, I read him as not involved in this.'

'Still makes no sense,' Mitch pointed out. 'Why would Lariquett want to have his own bookkeeper murdered. I mean, if Jacques knows about the extra money Lariquett is siphoning off of the profits, where is his motive for killing Donny?'

'That's the real mystery,' Jared admitted. 'First order of business is to get a line on the phony gunman who sullied Wyatt's name. He may be able to provide us with the information we need.'

'Good luck, Jared,' Mitch said. 'Let me know if you need me for anything.'

CHAPTER NINE

Gloria Jackson was past her prime and had played cards most of her adult life. Jared located her room on the upstairs floor of Ruby's Room and Lodge and woke her up with a concentrated pounding at her door.

Clad in a heavy, bright-colored robe and worn slippers, the woman was two score or more in age and there were traces of gray mixed in with her otherwise frizzled black hair. She had a haggard look without any paint to cover the flaws in her wrinkled face. With weary, dark-circled eyes, both from lack of sleep and a profession that included too much smoke and drink, she greeted him with a hoarse voice and an unmistakable coolness of demeanor. 'Whadda' you want?'

'Gloria Jackson,' Jared announced firmly. 'I believe you also go by the name of Glory Gold and Della Jones.'

Suspicion and fear flooded her features. 'Who are you? What's this about?'

Jared showed her his badge. 'Deputy US marshal Jared Valeron, ma'am. I think we should talk.'

Gloria reluctantly stepped back, opened the door wide enough for him to pass, and closed the door behind him.

Jared was surprised to find the cubical neat and tidy. There was a small sofa and chair on one side of the room, so he wandered over to stand at the chair and waited until she had sat down.

'Can I offer you a drink?' the woman asked.

'I'm not much of a drinking man,' he replied, removing his hat. Then he pulled the paper from inside his shirt and held it out to her.

'What's this?' she wanted to know.

'Take a look at the drawing. Tell me if you remember him.'

Gloria glanced at the sketch and sucked in an involuntary breath of air. Her eyes could not hide the fact she recognized the man. She hesitated, so Jared continued with the inquiry.

'You and I are standing at a fork in the road, Miss Jackson,' he informed her curtly. 'You tell me what you know about this man; tell me why you lost five hundred dollars to him; and I might overlook the outstanding warrant I have for your arrest.'

She lowered her eyes shamefully. 'I didn't know he was a killer. I only did what I was told.'

'Told by whom?'

'Rizzo. He dictates to me and Ron when we are to lose money, along with how much and to what person. It's usually once a week each. For our part, we sign the pay vouchers that show we didn't earn as much as we took in for the night.'

'And where does that extra money go?'

'I never asked,' she sighed. 'Lariquett allows us enough money to pay for room and board, along with a little spending money. We simply do as we are told.'

'And paying off a man to kill Donny Duval?'

'I had no idea the man was going to do that. Donny seemed like a nice young man.'

'How about the death listed on your wanted poster?'

'That wasn't my fault!' she blurted out. 'It was a card game that got out of hand. No one was supposed to get hurt!'

'You were caught cheating,' he reminded her.

'Yes, but I offered to give back the money and leave town. There was no need for violence.'

'A man died protecting your . . . um,' he searched for the right words. 'I guess we can't call it your honor, not when you were cheating.'

'The loser that night was drunk and mean. He wanted to strip me down to my drawers and run me out of town with nothing – no clothes, no money, nothing!'

'So a gentleman stood up for you and was killed for his trouble.'

Tears glistened in her eyes. 'I didn't want it to happen. When the fellow was shot, I ran. I escaped out the back and grabbed my things. I was gone before the law could catch me.'

'And you ended up here, a dealer working for Lariquett,' Jared postulated.

'Yes. Having been a saloon owner, Lariquett knew about my past. He used that knowledge to make me into one of his willing servants. Ron took a job under the same circumstances, being that he is wanted for wounding a deputy sheriff after being caught running a crooked game.'

'So, the extra money you earned for Lariquett? You never got a percentage of it?'

She laughed mockingly at the notion. 'We barely collect enough to live. With Ron Glover and I both having outstanding warrants, we do what we are told.'

'Tell me about this guy, the man who killed Donny Duval.'

Gloria looked again at the drawing and rotated her head from side to side. 'I don't know anything about him. The man said the right word and I made sure to let him win five hundred dollars. Soon as he was ahead the full amount, he cashed out. Next thing, I saw Rizzo speak to him, and he walked over to Ron's table. It didn't take long for him to win an equal amount a second time. As far as I know, he didn't interact with anyone else. He simply took his winnings and left the casino.'

'The man didn't mention where he came from or where he was going?'

'No.'

'Who told you to let him win?'

'Rizzo. He's always the one who gives us our orders. This was the first time I was asked to lose so much to a stranger I'd never seen before.'

'How did he describe the man?' Jared queried. 'I mean, how did you know which man was the one who expected to win?'

Gloria thought for a moment. 'Rizzo said the gentleman would be wearing black, and he had a pock-marked face. He would introduce himself with a single word – Sutter.'

'Do you think that was his name?'

'I have no idea. The guy pulled a chair at my table, said the word and handed me twenty dollars for chips. I began to deal and made sure he won the amount I was told.'

'Why not just hand him five hundred in chips?'

'It had to look as if he actually won the money. Mr Adour sometimes hires a watcher, a guy who keep tabs on who is winning or losing in the casino. The agreement between Lariquett and Ron and me is private. Other than Rizzo telling us when to lose, no one else knows about it. Adour is supposed to remain ignorant about the extra money that is skimmed off from our earnings.'

'His accountant has already informed him of the suspicious loses. That might come back to bite you and Ron.'

'It isn't us! It's Lariquett. He thinks he should be a partner, so he takes extra money. I don't know, maybe he is sticking it away in case he decides to pull stakes or something. It's none of my business.'

'This Sutter character, any idea where he came from or went?'

'No, as soon as he had the agreed upon winnings, he left my table.'

'The man at the hotel said he only spent one night. He came in by rail one day and left the next.'

Gloria grew thoughtful. 'I did notice one thing,' she mused. 'Like I said, the guy spoke to Rizzo after he had finished at my table. When Rizzo directed him to Ron's table, I got the feeling the two of them knew one another.'

'Rizzo strikes me as tight-lipped. I doubt he'd give me any information, especially if he was the one who sent for the gunman in the first place.' Then Jared had a thought. 'What can you tell me about the telegraph operator?'

'Parker James?' She frowned. 'He's an old bachelor. He runs the post and the telegraph office. Like most everyone else in town, Lariquett is the one who hired him.'

Jared figured he had learned as much as he could from

the lady gambler. He rose to his feet, his hat in his hand.

'I'd like to keep this visit private, Miss Jackson. Can I trust you to not say anything?'

She stood up as well. 'I doubt Rizzo or Mr Lariquett would approve. I'll keep it to myself, unless someone saw you enter the building.'

'I was careful.'

'And what about the warrant?'

'If things happened as you claim, my brother can probably get the hand bill called in. I'll talk to him after I finish here and see what he can do.'

The promise caused the woman's face to light up. 'Really? You would do that for me?'

'You seem basically honest, ma'am, and most professional gamblers cheat when they can get away with it. So, if you've been truthful with me, I'll try and see you get a second chance.'

She grabbed his hand with both of her own. 'That would be such a wonderful thing, Mr Valeron!' she exclaimed. 'I mean, truly wonderful.'

'Might take a few weeks,' he admitted. 'I'll see Brett when this job is over. I'm sure he can help.'

'Thank you!' she gushed, barely containing her gratitude. 'Thank you so much!'

Lariquett stormed about his office. 'Of all of the dumb, idiotic morons! Where did you find that bumbling clown? Couldn't even kill a sleeping man in his bed!'

'Valeron wasn't in his bed,' Rizzo excused the botched murder attempt. 'The crafty mongrel bedded down on the floor. Blake had no chance after he'd fired both barrels of the twelve-gauge – Valeron killed him deader than your shoe leather.'

'We just hired the man to work nights! Someone is likely to blab they've seen Blake before!'

'The guy cleaned up at nights and did a few odd jobs,' Rizzo argued. 'Hardly anyone knew about his past. He's only been working here a few days.'

'Out of the Boulder jail for less than a week and the man's killed while bushwhacking a Valeron in his hotel room. We can't hide that fact for long.'

'What can we do?'

Lariquett gave the matter some thought. 'Valeron being here is bringing trouble to our quiet little town. He's been asking questions, pushing people around snooping into things that aren't his business. Now a man has been killed, all because of his presence.' He grunted. 'It's time you and the boys ran him out of town.'

Rizzo gave him a double-take. 'Run Valeron out of Quick-Silver?'

'He's been nothing but trouble. Send him packing – preferably on the first train headed to Boulder.'

His number one man swallowed hard. 'What if he won't go?'

'There's three of you and only one of him. He isn't going to stand up and fight against three men!'

'I don't know, Chief.' Rizzo could not hide his apprehension. 'If we push him too hard, it will make him twice as suspicious. You sure we want him knowing you gave this order?'

'What order?' Lariquett asked, feigning innocence. 'The man has killers on his trail. One of them tried to murder him in his sleep. We don't want gunfights or killing in our town. That ought to be reason enough to send him packing.'

The man at the telegraph office was something of a rebel, wearing the gray pants and hat from the war. Aged and wrinkled, he had a face that looked like it needed ironing. Few teeth remained in his mouth and his bulb nose showed a redness from heavy drinking.

'Whatta yuh say, old-timer?' Jared greeted him. 'Still waitin' for the South to rise again?'

The man had a natural squint, but spoke in a mellow tone. 'It's a comin', youngster. You just wait and see.'

Jared laughed. 'I haven't been called "youngster" for some time.'

He grinned. 'Everyone is a youngster to me. I'll be seventy-five this winter.'

'Man oh mama! you were well along in years during the war.'

He snorted his contempt. 'Bunch of ignorant yahoos, about didn't let me fight. I set them straight about it and made sissies out of half the men in uniform. Walked into my first battle as a private and come out with an armload of stripes.'

'How'd you end up here?'

'The he-bull, Adour, being French, was sympathetic to the South. He signed off on me when Lariquett offered me the job of telegrapher and managing the post. I also fill-in as a Faro dealer on occasion, when Lariquett is short-handed.'

Jared got down to business. 'I need to send a wire so I can ask about a feller. Problem is, I'm not quite sure about the name.'

'The name of who you're sending the message to?'

'No, the one I'm asking about.'

Parker laughed. 'You ain't gonna get much of an answer if you don't even know the question.'

'I think it's Sutter or something like that. Do you recall sending a message to someone with that name?'

Parker pulled out a journal and opened it up. 'I list all of the messages sent or received – orders of Mr Lariquett. How long ago would this be?'

'A couple of weeks, near as I know.'

'I've got a Sutherland here.' He frowned. 'Naw, wouldn't be him, he's a regular – supplies us with tools and such.' He continued through the list.

'Ah-hah!' he exclaimed. 'Here's the one I'll bet you're looking for – Sutterfield. Nothing else, just Sutterfield.'

'How did you reach him?'

'Rizzo told me he could be reached through the Denver office. I don't recall much else. Rizzo dictated the words and I sent them. Next day I get an answer that does stand out in my mind – exactly two letters: O and K.'

Jared thanked the man and sent his inquiry to Sergeant Fielding.

'I didn't know you were asking about this guy just so you could set the police on him.'

'No, it isn't like that,' Jared replied. 'I need to talk to the man, and the only person I know in Denver is one of the lawmen there. Him being a policeman, he can check their records and maybe help me locate Sutterfield.'

The old boy was still frowning, so Jared pulled out a ten-dollar gold piece. 'I appreciate your help, old-timer. Have a few drinks on me.'

Money meant more to the man than gratitude. He

smiled wide enough to show all six of his remaining teeth.

'Good doing business with you, youngster. Anything else you need, just give a holler.'

'I'll keep it in mind . . . and thanks for your trouble.'

Crystal had washed her hair and was in the midst of combing it dry when a knock came at her door. She muttered a mild oath and opened it.

Mitch was standing there, clean clothes, freshly shaven, his hair neatly groomed, with a small bouquet of flowers in his hand.

'Mitch!' Crystal lamented, unhappy at being caught in the middle of a personal chore. 'What are you doing here at this time of day? I'm busy washing my hair.'

'I won't take but a moment of your time, Miss Crystal,' he said, displaying a puppy-dog meekness. 'I have to get something straight in my mind.'

She put her hands on her hips and looked at the flowers. 'Are those for me?'

He gave her a helpless look. 'It's all I could find. No one sells flowers in town, but I managed to get these from the Adour garden.'

'You approached Mrs Adour and asked to pick her flowers?'

'Well, actually, it was Coleen Adour, her sister-in-law. She was right happy to help me. She pretty much chose the ones so they would make a proper bouquet.'

Taking the offered flowers, Crystal raised them to her face and tested the scent. 'Very nice,' she gave her approval. 'But why the flowers? We haven't set a time or date for another outing.'

Mitch took a deep breath, as if drawing in his courage.

Then he blundered out, 'Jared said I ought to face up to you like a man.'

Crystal's brow lifted in surprise. 'You're taking advice from a confirmed "I'll-never-get-married bachelor?" ' She laughed at the notion. 'You do realize Jared is about as awkward around a woman as he would be trying to pick out a pair of bloomers for his mother?'

Mitch squirmed. 'Yeah, but you and him . . . The two of you kissed and. . . .' He floundered like a fish out of water. 'I mean, are you. . . ?' Summoning his bravado, he blurted: 'Have you got your heart set on him?'

Crystal didn't laugh, although she could not prevent humor from shining brightly in her eyes. 'Jared has been like a . . . a big brother to me,' she said lightly. 'However, he's made it quite clear that he would make a terrible husband.'

When Mitch didn't say anything, she placed the flowers on the table and turned toward the single window in the room. 'I've got to get a little breeze for my hair or it'll never dry.'

She opened the window to allow in some fresh air, but gasped. 'Mitch!' she cried. 'Look what's going on down in the street! My dead Lord! This can't be happening!'

CHAPTER TEN

Jared was unprepared for the face-off. Rizzo, Blade and Keogh were spread across his path. Blade was sporting a shotgun, while Rizzo and Keogh both had a hand resting on the butt of their guns.

'You're running me out of town?' Jared was stunned at the order.

'We're charged with keeping the peace, Valeron,' Rizzo stated firmly. 'You killed a man in the hotel.' He raised his free hand to stop Jared from speaking. 'Now, we know your action was in self-defense, but the fact remains that guy came looking for you. Might have been other people hurt in your personal fight – innocent people. A bullet goes through walls or windows, stray bullets kill or injure people all of the time.'

Jared scrutinized the trio, weighing the odds against survival should this come to a shootout. Quick as he was with his gun, he knew even Wyatt would have chosen to talk rather than have drawn his gun in this situation.

'I'm not looking to stick around your upstanding community more than a few days, Rizzo. If you would give me a little help finding the man who hired Donny's killer, it could shorten my stay.'

'You're howling at the moon, champ. There's nothing to find. A wandering show-off with a gun pushed Donny into a fight. That's all there is to it.'

'You aren't much good at lying, Rizzo,' Jared countered. 'His murder was neither a show-off wanting a thrill, nor a man looking for a reputation. It was an execution, plain and simple.'

'So says you.'

'So says his sister,' Jared avowed. 'And that's good enough for me.'

Rizzo glowered at Jared, obviously not eager to push him further, yet unable to back away. A handful of people had stopped to watch, and more were gathering along the walks. What had begun as a warning, expecting the odds to convince Valeron to comply with their get-out-of-town order, had become a dangerous confrontation.

'We don't want any more killing,' Rizzo hissed through gritted teeth. 'Don't let your pride overrule your good sense.'

'And don't you think you can bully Jared or anyone helping me to find my brother's killer!' The declaration came from the nearby walkway.

Crystal was holding a gun with both hands, pointing it at Rizzo! She had the hammer cocked back and had taken aim at him.

'I mean what I say, Rizzo!' her voice rose an octave from the strain of the moment. 'You try running Mr Valeron out of town and I'll put you down like a rabid dog!'

Rizzo took a step back, shocked to see Crystal's unwavering muzzle pointed at him. Both Blade and Keogh looked confused, needing guidance. This was not sup-posed to end in a gunfight, especially one with a woman involved! Before another word or action could be taken, two men walked up to join Jared, one stopping at either side. They both had their hands resting on their guns.

'What's going on, Jer?' Shane asked, eyeing the trio blocking the street. 'You got some excitement for us?'

'Yeah,' Cliff chipped in. 'You weren't thinking of having sport with these fellas and not inviting us to the party.'

Jared allowed an assured grin to spread across his lips. 'Rizzo, meet two of my cousins − Shane and Cliff. And you don't want to underestimate Miss Duval either. She's a pretty fair shot. We've been practicing together since we met. I'll bet a dime to your dollar she could plug you dead center before your gun clears leather.'

Rizzo lifted his hand carefully away from his gun, sud-denly overcome with a desire to find a peaceful solution. Blade lowered the scatter-gun, while Keogh also moved his hand away from his gun.

'We're not looking for a gun battle,' Rizzo said, backing water. 'It's our job to keep the peace.'

'And a good job you do, too,' Jared replied. 'Other than when you allowed a gunman to shoot down Donny Duval in cold blood. Where were you then?'

'Can't hold that against us,' he muttered weakly. 'There was no warning, no way for us to know the guy was out to kill anyone. By the time we learned of the shooting, the man was gone.'

'How does a murderer arrive and leave the town of Quick-Silver without you even talking to him? From what I've learned, after the yellow maggot killed Donny he ambled down to the train station and casually left for

Boulder. You didn't do an ounce of investigating. . . .' Jared's voice grew cold, 'And that bespeaks of collusion. I'm guessing you knew the guy and the exact reason he came to town.'

'Now wait a minute, Valeron! You got no call to accuse me of something like that.'

'Explain it to me, Rizzo,' Jared challenged. 'Make me believe you aren't a conspirator in Donny's death.'

'Yes!' Crystal cried, still holding her gun on the man. 'I'm waiting for your answer! Why did you let the murderer of my brother leave town without questioning him?'

Rizzo took another step backward. How quickly the odds had changed. From three against one to four against three, and one of them a grief-stricken woman who might pull the trigger at any second.

'It was a mistake, OK?' Rizzo threw out the words. 'By the time we figured out what had happened, the train was gone.'

'A telegraph message to the law at Boulder would have been enough to stop and hold the man for questioning,' Jared pointed out. 'You did nothing.'

Rizzo hated seeing the curious and suspicious looks of the spectators. Rather than stumble through one excuse after another, he took the coward's way out.

'This meeting is over,' he grunted sourly. 'You've been warned, Valeron. Don't be getting into any more trouble. If you've got a beef with someone, you come to me first.'

Jared laughed dryly. 'Count on it, Rizzo. I'm betting I'll be around to see you real soon.'

As the three cowed men retreated, Jared shook hands with Cliff and Shane. Then he led them over to meet Crystal. She had put her gun into a dress pocket and greeted them with a hesitant smile.

'So this gal about blew out your candle, huh?' Shane teased. 'Never figured your end would come at the hand of a pretty girl.'

Cliff chuckled his agreement. 'Yeah, I thought I was the one who would be shot by an angry female.'

Jared introduced them all around as Mitch came out of the store to join them. He lifted his shoulders in a helpless gesture. 'What could I do, Jared? I came courting, so I didn't have my gun. Plus, I knew better than to try and stop Crystal. She'd have never spoken to me again if I didn't let her try to help you.'

'Getting out of her way shows you have a degree of intelligence, Mitch,' Jared allowed.

'So,' Crystal said, trying to save Mitch's manly pride, 'these are two more Valerons?'

'Cliff is a Mason, one of our cousins,' Jared informed her. 'Shane is one of my two uncles' boys. The three of us have worked together a few times in the past.'

Mitch stepped forward to shake hands with both men, while Crystal simply gave each of them a diminutive nod.

'I didn't expect to see you boys,' Jared spoke to Shane. 'Why are you and Cliff here?'

'Cliff offered his prowess with a gun,' Shane answered. 'Me, I'm here because Brett doesn't want you misusing your deputy's badge.'

'Misusing?'

'You know, like hanging a couple guys without a trial. He doesn't want your actions to reflect poorly on his decision to let you carry that badge around.'

'Who's Brett?' Crystal wanted to know.

'My younger brother,' Jared clarified.

'I thought Nash was your younger brother,' she said.

'I've got three brothers, little lady – every one of them sticklers for the law.'

'You're lucky he sent me and Cliff,' Shane tossed out. 'At least, we won't arrest you if you cross the line.'

'Funny man,' Jared griped.

'Where can we get something to eat?' Cliff wanted to know. 'Me and Shane left before breakfast this morning. That narrow-gauge train is even more uncomfortable than the one from Cheyenne.'

Jared looked at Crystal and Mitch. 'You two up for an early lunch? It'll give you a chance to get acquainted with my cousins.'

'Let me put away my gun and run a brush through my hair,' Crystal said. 'Ten minutes?'

'Mitch,' Jared spoke to the blacksmith. 'How about you hang back and escort Crystal to the eatery? We'll go on ahead and get a table for the five of us.'

Rizzo stood with his hat in his hand, shoulders bowed with his failure.

'Of all the blasted foul-ups!' Lariquett roared. 'Valeron made fools of you three in front of the whole town.'

'It ain't like we planned it that way, Chief. Crystal come flying out of her apartment with a gun in her hand. Then two of Valeron's kin showed up.' He heaved a sigh. 'We had no chance. If we'd have tried anything, we'd have been face down in pools of our own blood.'

Lariquett waved his hand to end the fiasco. 'It's done. There's nothing we can do about it now.'

'This is getting serious. Now we've got three Valeron men to deal with.'

'They still have nothing on us,' Lariquett maintained. 'No one is going to discover the motive behind Donny's killing, and it's going to stay that way.'

'I don't know, Chief,' Rizzo said. 'Valeron is a one hellish hunting dog. If he ever gets the scent, we're in for a fight. And with the odds being purtin-near even, I don't see us coming out of this with a whole skin.'

'You going yellow on me?'

Rizzo snapped erect, his face a resolute mask. 'You know me better than that, Andy. I've been with you too long for you to ask such a question.'

Lariquett softened his stance. Rizzo never called him by name unless it was something extremely personal.

'All right, Rizzo,' he excused his remark. 'I didn't mean that.'

Rizzo relaxed. 'What I see here is us being over our heads on this. These are the Valerons. They have a reputation for never quitting. Plus, we used Sutter to get rid of Donny and lost Blake at the hotel. Those are the only two guns I had to back our play. Blade and Keogh are good men, but we no longer have the advantage.'

'Maybe we could hire a couple more guns.'

'To go up against the Valerons?' Rizzo laughed in a mocking tone. 'If I wasn't being paid top wages . . . and your friend, I wouldn't be sticking around.'

'Then we will stay on this course. We've left no loose ends, no way for Valeron to learn anything. Even if Gloria or Ron were to talk, they don't know anything of value. Plus there's nothing to connect us to Donny's killer. I can explain away any amount of money Jacques might find missing, to go for some needed for improvements or supplies for the casino. We stick to the story – Sutter was a

115

man I hired to earn a few dollars for expenses. I couldn't have known he was a killer, that he would choose a random person on the street and push them into a gun-fight.'

'That works,' Rizzo gave his approval. 'He was a stranger we hired to collect a few bucks by winning at cards. We used the money for new equipment and paid him fifty bucks for his trouble. How could we have known he was a crazy, wannabe gunman?'

'Exactly. Keep everything normal and, in good time, Valeron will be forced to give up. Crystal will have to accept her brother's death was a case of bad luck, that it meant nothing to any of us.'

'OK, Chief,' Rizzo concurred, able to grin once more. 'This new strategy beats the daylights out of me and the boys taking on a trio of Valerons.'

Having extra bodies to work with did little to solve the mystery in Quick-Silver. Rizzo and his thugs pretty much ignored Jared and the others. Worse, Gloria and Ron cornered Jared one afternoon. They told him Rizzo had admitted the murderer, Sutter, had been hired to win money for Lariquett. The reason given was he intended to buy a new roulette wheel and needed the extra money. Supposedly, Adour had nixed the expenditure when asked, so Lariquett was going around him.

Jared joined Crystal, Mitch and his cousins that very night at the eating house. While waiting to be served, he told them about the meeting.

'Is there a chance those two are telling it straight?' Mitch asked Jared.

'Whether or not they actually believe it, I'd say it's the

story we're stuck with.'

'It's a jelly jar full of sand!' Crystal ranted. 'You can't seriously believe a stranger would challenge a mild-mannered, lowly bookkeeper to a gunfight for the fun of killing a man.' She fought to keep her voice down, 'He knew Donny's name! Someone hired Sutter to murder him!'

'You have talked to these two dealers,' Shane plied the question to Jared. 'What's your take?'

'I'd call it convenient,' Cliff put in his ante before Jared could reply.

'Lariquett made it up!' Crystal insisted, also preventing Jared from getting in a word. 'It's a thick fog he's created to keep us from finding out the truth.'

'This came for you a few minutes ago,' Shane intervened in the heated discussion to hand Jared a message. 'The Southern gent who runs the telegraph said he knew you would want it right away.'

'Pays to tip the right people,' Jared said, taking the paper and pausing to read it.

'Who is the man you're looking for?' Shane asked, knowing what was in the telegram. 'And why did Sergeant Fielding track him down for you?'

'His name is Sutterfield, and I'm pretty sure he's the one who gunned down Donny.'

'What?' Crystal cried – causing a good many customers in the room to look in her direction. She lowered her head and her voice at once, but did not hide her excitement. 'You've found Donny's killer?'

'Yes,' Jared replied. 'But I doubt he knows why he was hired. A stinkpot gunnie, offered a thousand dollars to force someone into a fight? He isn't necessarily going to ask for details.'

'So much for the story about a new roulette wheel,' Cliff grunted.

Jared agreed, 'Like the little lady says, it's a cover for the truth.'

Crystal pounded her fists on the table. 'This is maddening! We know who the killer is, but still have no idea as to why he murdered Donny!'

'How you going to prove anything?' Mitch chipped in a sour remark. 'Like you said, Sutter . . . or Sutterfield, probably doesn't know or care why Donny was the target.'

Jared took a hard look at Crystal. 'You said you wanted the man who murdered your brother to die a similar death.' At her nod, he continued. 'If he's the one who did the shooting, I can put the swine in a box.'

She realized what he was suggesting. 'Not without me,' she made a quiet oath. 'I stood by, completely helpless, and watched that animal shoot my brother.'

'I don't see how this will help find the answers we're looking for,' Shane restated the imbroglio. 'The extra money has been explained; maybe Sutter did act on his own when he killed the lady's brother. Unless we find something, or someone, to tell us different, we're at a dead end.'

The meal arrived and the serious talk was abandoned to keep the food from getting cold. After everyone had pretty much finished, Jared returned to their dilemma.

'The way I see it, our next chore is to run down this Sutter character. If he can shed light on who ordered Donny killed, we might have to turn him over to the law.' Before Crystal could object, he hurried on. 'However, it would be on the condition he testify against the man who hired him to do the job.'

'Then he would get off with a few years in prison!' the girl snapped angrily. 'He would never pay the full price for killing my brother!'

Jared placed his hand over her own. 'I said "if", Crystal. I doubt very much that Sutter can tell us more than who offered him the job . . . and that is probably going to be Rizzo.'

Mitch snorted his contempt. 'Good luck trying to get Rizzo to give up Lariquett. He's been with him for several years and is as loyal as a hound dog.'

'I read him the same way, too,' Jared admitted. 'There is a possibility of some outside help, but I'm not sure how to go about getting it.'

Crystal stared at Jared as if he were speaking in a foreign language. 'You aren't making any sense. Outside help? What are you talking about?'

'It's a long shot, little lady,' he confessed. 'Kind of a last resort if we hit the dead end Shane mentioned.'

'What about Sutter?' she wanted to know. 'I refuse to let him get away with murder!'

Shane chuckled at her outburst. 'That's already been decided, miss.'

When she looked at Shane, he expounded: 'Unless the guy confesses his crime to the law, Jer is gonna force him to fight.'

'But . . . but he said. . . .'

'Sutter might give up Rizzo, but he probably has no idea as to the big dog we're after.' Cliff made his own deduction. 'The guy will have to draw against Jerry.'

'What if he's faster than you?' Crystal pinned Jared down. 'You can't be certain he won't be the one to kill you!'

'That's why I'm taking you along,' Jared said easily. 'You're my back-up. If he gets me, you fulfill your vow to shoot him . . . for both your brother's sake and mine!'

Rizzo entered the room to discover Lariquett had a girl on his lap. Shocked by the intrusion, she pulled back from kissing him and jumped to her feet. Andrew frowned at Rizzo, but he had forgotten to lock the door, so it was his own mistake.

'Excuse us, Trixie,' he apologized to her. 'We'll continue our conversation later.'

The girl scurried from the room and Rizzo flashed a salacious grin. 'Good thing I wasn't ten minutes later, Chief. Could have been embarrassing for all three of us.'

'I'll be sure and lock the door next time I need some privacy,' Lariquett avowed. 'What brings you to the office?'

'Parker bypassed the usual procedure and gave a telegraph message to Valeron . . . without my seeing it first.'

'That diehard johnny-reb! He never has learned to take orders worth a damn.'

'Too bad Adour approved of hiring him – he can ignore the rules we have in place.'

'Did he tell you what was in the message?'

'Yeah, but it didn't make a lot of sense,' Rizzo outlined. 'It was only two words: "Found him", and it was signed Fielding.'

'Did you ask Parker about this Fielding?'

'He never heard of him until Valeron had him send his wire.'

'What wire?' Lariquett demanded to know. 'You never told me he sent any telegraph messages.'

Rizzo lifted his shoulders in a helpless gesture. 'Parker

claimed it slipped his mind.'

Lariquett swore. 'So who is this Fielding?'

'No idea, Chief.'

'Fielding. . . ? Denver. . . ? 'Lariquett rubbed his temples in frustration. 'But it did say this guy had found someone.'

Rizzo gravely lowered his head. 'I've a bad feeling, Chief. I'll bet that there wire is telling Valeron who and where Sutter is at.'

'Impossible!' he growled. 'The man came in, did his job, and left. He was a ghost. No one even knows his real name.'

'I told you Sutter made a mistake claiming to be a Valeron. I hope my old riding companion had a good time and spent all the money you paid him, cause I reckon he's going to be staring at the inside of a box in a coupla days.'

'Did you give Gloria and Ron the story about the new roulette wheel I ordered?'

'Yep. I confirmed that much.' Rizzo shrugged. 'Guess Valeron didn't buy it.'

'Why do you say that?'

' 'Cause Valeron and the Duval gal took the afternoon train to Boulder.'

Lariquett felt the inside of his stomach roil, and his heart beat began to race. He could not remain seated and began to pace around the room to relieve the pent-up emotions. Rizzo remained a fixture, awaiting his sage advice. After two circles, Lariquett stopped at his office window and looked out upon the street.

'What about the two new men who joined up with Valeron? Did they go with him?'

'One of them tagged along – the other stayed here.'

'If one of them is sticking around, it means Valeron still intends to find out who hired Sutter.'

'Ain't no chance of that, Chief,' Rizzo jeered. 'You and me are the only ones who know about my ex-pard. As for Sutter, he don't know you even exist.'

'Need I remind you that bloodhound managed to track down your friend. How on earth did he manage that feat?'

Rizzo gave his head a shake. 'Durned if I know. Sutter did exactly what I told him to do. He used a phony name at the hotel and didn't say ten words in the twenty-four hours he was here. There ain't a man in town who would have recognized him, and the two of us didn't speak, except when I directed him to Gloria and Ron's tables.'

'Contact Deloss Reed in Denver. If this ends up before a judge, he will know how to handle it.'

'Deloss is a shrewd gent,' Rizzo approved of the idea. 'I'll include a few details so he knows what we need.'

'Promise him a good fee for his work. If Valeron kills Sutter outright, there's nothing we can do. But if he lets the law handle it. . . .'

Rizzo guffawed. 'Deloss will get him a stroll down freedom road!'

'Send the telegraph message off right away, and tell Parker to keep his damn mouth shut about this wire. After you're finished with that, tell Blade and Keogh to keep on their toes. I doubt there will be any trouble at our end, but we need to keep a sharp eye.'

'Right you are, Chief. We've no worries about this whole thing, 'cause there ain't one loose end anyone will ever find.'

'True words, my friend,' Lariquett professed. 'Nothing has changed. We are still untouchable.'

*

By the time Jared, Cliff and Crystal reached Denver, it was full dark. They stopped at the Grand Hotel and got rooms for the night. Then they found a restaurant and ordered a meal. Crystal was too nervous to eat more than a few bites. Being so close to her goal, she could hardly sit still.

'I need to speak to Sergeant Fielding,' Jared announced his intentions. 'He will know where we can find Sutter.'

Abruptly, Crystal reached across the table and took hold of Jared's hand. He gave her a curious look, wondering why she had such a grim expression. 'What?' he asked.

'I. . . .' she couldn't seem to get her words started. 'Jared, I've been giving this idea a great deal of thought. And I worry. . . .'

'We'll find Sutter,' he voiced his confidence.

'No,' she murmured softly. 'I mean, maybe it would be enough to put him behind bars. I can testify how he forced Donny to try and defend himself – it was an outright act of murder. If a judge gives him a long sentence, you wouldn't have to risk your life.'

'This is what you wanted, Crystal,' Jared reminded her. 'To see this man punished for killing your brother in front of your eyes.'

'What if he is faster than you or gets off a lucky shot?' she worried. 'I would never forgive myself if I got you wounded or killed. You've been such a strong supporter for me. Gentle. Compassionate. Exactly like Donny.'

Jared smiled. 'Durned if you aren't twisting a knot around my heart, little lady. I'm proud as a prize bull at a county fair that you are looking after my welfare, but I can take this character with no sweat.' She opened her mouth to say something, but he added: 'And, don't forget why I'm here. This craven snake disgraced Wyatt's good name. I'd have tracked him down even if you wanted no part of this.'

Her scrutiny was enough to cause a saloon dancer to blush, searching for any hint of deception. After a long peruse, Crystal removed her hand from his. 'You really mean that?'

'I'm honor-bound to clear Wyatt's name,' Jared confirmed. 'My cousin never killed a man who wasn't trying to kill him right back. He is as honorable as the day is long. Every breath this Sutterfield takes is an added insult.'

'With Wyatt being such a good man, wouldn't he prefer you to try and put this guy behind bars, rather than kill him in a gunfight?'

'It's like we agreed. I'll offer him the choice – confess, or be put in the ground.'

Cliff had been silent throughout the verbal exchange. 'Back to getting this chore done, where do we find Fielding?' He showed a smirk. 'And how much help will he be once you tell him what you have in mind?'

'He may have balked at me calling Sutter out without giving the man any options. With our willingness to accept a surrender for the killer's testimony, he won't get in the way.'

However, the following morning, when the three of them were in a private office at the police station, Sergeant Fielding was unwilling to sanction any kind of deadly confrontation. He was firmly determined to do this by the book . . . and he meant the Book of Law.

'Dad-gum, Fielding!' Jared complained. 'After all the

help you've gotten from me and my family. And now you want us to stand by idly while you make the arrest?'

'Quick-Silver is in Colorado, Jared. The man is in my city. It's my duty to arrest him and take him before a judge.'

Cliff spoke up, 'Jared is packing a Deputy US marshal's badge. Don't that make it his responsibility to arrest Sutterfield?'

'The US Marshal's office only steps in when the local authorities can't handle the situation. This is a murder-for-hire killing. It's our job.'

'What if a judge doesn't see this my way?' Crystal erupted. 'What if he declares that, because Donny was wearing a gun, this was a fair gunfight and not murder?'

Fielding groaned his frustration. 'For the love of Heaven! I am not a magistrate, I'm a policeman. I can't be held accountable for what a judge may or may not do.'

'So let Jerry make the arrest,' Cliff argued. 'If Sutterfield draws against a lawman, he deserves to end up a corpse in a coffin. If not, then you can put the man in front of a judge.'

'Look,' Fielding made an entreaty, 'I found the guy for you. I know where he hangs his hat. I can make this arrest with no gunplay. Let me do my job.'

'And if your judge gives him a slap on the backside and turns him loose?' Jared challenged.

Fielding grunted. 'Then, I'd appreciate it if you'd make sure he isn't within Denver's city limits when you confront him.'

Jared turned his attention to Crystal. 'It looks like this is the route we're taking. Are you OK with it?'

Before she could respond, there came a sharp knock,

causing all eyes to focus on the door. It opened and Officer Munsen stepped into the room.

'Pardon me, Sarge,' he said, displaying a pronounced puzzlement, 'but a guy just turned himself in at the front desk.'

'Why are you telling me?'

Munsen frowned. 'Because it's the fellow you asked to have named in a warrant – Sutterfield?'

CHAPTER ELEVEN

Donny's murderer was attired in a freshly pressed black suit, a brand new hat, and wore a smug disdain on his face. Standing next to him, immaculately dressed in a professionally tailored tan suit and bowler hat, was a lean fellow of average height. He had the black, darting eyes of a weasel, complete with a narrow, pointed nose and a neatly trimmed mustache. The smile upon his lips was as pious and superior as if he had been elected First Pig at the feeding troughs.

'Word has reached Mr Sutterfield that a warrant has been issued for his arrest,' the musteline gent spouted off. 'I am Deloss Reed, Attorney at Law, and this man is my client.'

Fielding ran a hand through his thinning hair. 'How is it that Sutterfield has a lawyer before the warrant has even been issued?'

'I keep abreast of such things, sir,' Deloss maintained his air of importance. 'It is my job to see that my client has his day in court. There is a rumor going round that he might be drawn into a duel or such thing before he can muster a judicial defense.'

'That walking dung-heap standing next to you murdered my brother!' Crystal charged. 'He didn't give him a chance!'

Deloss waved his hand in a defensive gesture. 'Do you hear that, officer?' he voiced his concern to Fielding. 'Does that sound like a person willing to await the decision of a judge and jury?'

'Fact remains, this man shot down a defenseless bookkeeper,' Fielding countered.

'And he slandered my cousin's name,' Jared added to his offenses. 'That's begging for a bullet in the teeth!'

'Unsubstantiated claims that must be proven in a court of law,' he spouted piously. 'I am here to see that no one interferes with Mr Sutterfield's right to a fair and impartial trial. It is why I accompanied him here, so as to ensure he is held in safe custody until a hearing can be arranged.'

'Officer Munsen,' Fielding spoke to his subordinate, 'see to it our guest is searched and given the best suite in the station.'

'I'd prefer to lock him in the outhouse,' Munsen grunted. But he took Sutterfield by the arm and led him down the hall to the block of cells.

Deloss glanced at Jared and sniffed odiously. 'I will see you and the lady in court. You will be notified as soon as the judge appoints a time for a hearing.'

'Who contacted you?' Jared demanded to know. 'How did you learn about the warrant?'

'A friend of my client . . . and that's all I have to say on the matter. I have been employed to defend Mr Sutterfield, and I shall do so to the best of my ability.'

The four of them watched as the man strode smartly out the front door. Cliff was the first to speak up.

'Something sure smells bad, Jerry. That fellow is a first cousin to the snake who tempted Eve.'

'I'm betting the three of you were seen leaving Quick-Silver,' Fielding guessed. 'Somebody wired ahead of you.'

'So much for your being able to confront Sutterfield and worm any information out of him,' Cliff expressed the obvious to Jared. 'And I'll bet that slick popinjay has already found a way to get him off the hook.'

'Lariquett covering his back,' Jared muttered. 'The guy has some smarts . . . and the contacts to boot.'

'Yeah, but how did he get an attorney so fast?' Cliff asked, regarding Fielding with an accusatory gaze.

'Don't be looking at me, sonny!' Fielding yelped. 'I barely had time to write out the arrest request. The judge hasn't even signed it yet!'

'It was expected,' Jared deduced. 'Because we brought Crystal with us, Lariquett knew we had found his hired killer.'

'And, naturally, the crooked, lowdown sidewinder has a sleazy rodent ready to do his bidding.'

'You don't think Deloss will get Sutterfield off?' Crystal asked. 'I mean, I heard the threat! I saw the shooting! How can anyone stop my getting justice for that?'

'Justice and the law are very different things,' Fielding admitted. 'Every new law put on the books for the last twenty years has been to protect the guilty, and it usually comes at the expense of the innocent victims.' He shook his head. 'Tell you one thing, that shifty-eyed lawyer didn't lack for confidence.'

'He must be figuring on declaring the shooting as self-defense,' Cliff suggested. 'After all, Miss Duval's brother was wearing a gun.'

'Which he never got out of its holster!' Crystal snapped. 'Besides, Sutterfield said he was going to kill him, no matter what! He forced Donny to try and defend himself.'

'Were there other witnesses to the shooting?' Jared wanted to know. 'Did anyone else hear what Sutterfield said to your brother?'

'I don't think so. It was early; there weren't many people on the street yet. I doubt anyone but me was close enough to pick up what was said.'

They continued discussing the bizarre turn of events for the next hour. Nothing new could be added and only a couple of contingencies were reached. The meeting was at an end when Munsen once more entered the room.

'You aren't going to believe this, Sarge,' he warned.

Everyone waited for him to continue. He didn't go on until Fielding prompted him with a 'Well?'

'We're to have Sutterfield in court at one o'clock for his hearing. The judge will determine if there is grounds for an actual trial.'

Fielding looked at a clock on the wall. 'Two hours?' he exclaimed. 'How the hell did that slick talkin' slug manage to talk the judge into a hearing this afternoon? We haven't yet gotten around to having the warrant signed for this guy's arrest!'

'Did I mention the stink emanating from this whole mess?' Cliff said. 'Week old fish don't smell any worse than this.'

The judge looked over the arrest request, glanced at the defendant, swept over the few spectators in the room, then rested his gaze on the city prosecuting attorney. He had been advised of the charges.

'Do you have any witnesses for this proceeding?'

The attorney nodded at Crystal. 'This is the sister of the man who was killed in Quick-Silver. She was with her brother at the time of the shooting.'

'Any others?'

'She is the only one who saw and heard exactly what transpired,' he answered.

Turning to the defendant's lawyer, 'And do you have any witnesses to call?'

'If it please the court,' Deloss announced, standing erect, his chin lifted high. 'I believe we can clear this up in a very short amount of time, Your Honor. I have four witnesses to present. They were involved in an all-night game of cards in the back room of Quincy's until the morning of the day in question. As Mr Sutterfield was the fifth player, it would have been impossible for him to have been in Quick-Silver for any shooting.'

The judge frowned at the news, then looked to Crystal. 'Are you absolutely certain this is the man you saw?'

Crystal jumped to her feet. 'He murdered my brother!' she cried. 'He stopped us on the street and told Donny he was going to shoot him whether he drew his gun or not!'

Rotating back to Deloss. 'And where are the four card players?

Deloss gestured to four men. All were wearing brand new suits, with fresh haircuts and shaves. They rose to their feet and stood there for inspection.

The judge's face darkened with a scowl. 'There isn't a one of those men I haven't had in my court for drunkenness or disorderly conduct, Mr Reed.'

'True, these gentlemen have all made mistakes in the past,' Deloss admitted. 'But they are well known at the poker tables and other games of chance. Each of them will swear that Mr Sutterfield was at the all-night game. In fact, Mr Sutterfield was actually the biggest loser during the night.'

'Enough to have provided a new suit of clothes for each man!' the prosecuting attorney howled his dismay. 'Your Honor, this is a complete travesty! These barflies would point the finger at their own mother for the price of a drink!'

'They are citizens of Denver,' the judge answered back.

'And this young lady had to watch as Mr Sutterfield menaced and tormented her brother, threatening to shoot him down whether he tried to defend himself or not! Donald Duval was a bookkeeper, with no history of violence, a non-drinking, non-gambling man. He was sought out and murdered for some unknown reason . . . by Mr Sutterfield!'

The judge tapped his gavel. 'That's enough!' he silenced the attorney. Then he composed himself and spoke solemnly. 'I am not blinded to the truth in this matter.' He looked at Crystal and regret shone brightly in his eyes.

'Is there anyone else who can corroborate your story, young lady?'

'No one who would dare speak up,' she replied. 'We believe the man who hired Sutterfield to kill my brother is the most powerful man in Quick-Silver. Anyone testifying would risk losing their job or their life.'

The judge glared at Deloss. 'If I ever learn you were a knowing party to this farce, I will see you never practice law again.'

The man's expression was one of affront. 'Your Honor,

I assure you. This is all completely above board.'

'Just heed the warning, counselor. Woe be unto you if you come before me with such an obvious ruse ever again.'

Deloss folded his arms and sat down next to his client.

The judge did not hide his ruefulness as he turned to Crystal. 'Justice is blind, we are told, and it is at such times I wish that weren't the case. I believe you are telling the truth, young lady . . . but the law does not recognize the truth, only the evidence presented. With four witnesses claiming Mr Sutterfield was here in Denver at the time of your brother's death, I have no choice but to declare him not guilty.'

He tapped his gavel and sighed, 'Case dismissed.'

Leaving the courthouse, Fielding offered his condolences and regret, then left the four of them to return to his station.

Crystal was devastated by the release of Sutterfield, but Jared patted her on the shoulder and displayed a confident smile. 'It's only one hand,' he consoled her. 'The game isn't over yet.'

'Holy jumpin' catfish!' Cliff complained. 'What are you talking about? We lost the case! Sutterfield is a free man!'

Crystal glowered at him as well. 'Yes, Jared. How can you be so cheery about Sutterfield getting away with murder?'

'You guys are looking at the fence, but you can't see the field beyond. This is a major break for our side.'

Both of Jared's companions stopped in the middle of the walk and gawked open-mouthed at his surreal statement.

'Explain,' Crystal said, recouping her aplomb.

Jared led her over to a nearby alleyway. Cliff tagged along until the three of them were out of sight from anyone on the street.

'All right,' Cliff voiced his impatience. 'Give, Cousin. What is it that Crystal and me are missing?'

'What's the one thing we've been searching for since Donny's murder?' he asked. Seeing both of their blank stares, he answered the question himself. 'A connection to the man who gave the order to have him killed!'

Cliff and Crystal exchanged looks, but neither of them grasped what they were missing.

'Amateurs,' Jared chided them. 'I'm working with utter greenhorn detectives.'

'Tell us!' Crystal demanded. 'What could possibly be good about Sutterfield being found not-guilty?'

Jared showed a wry grin. 'Someone hired Deloss. They paid big money for him to bribe those four witnesses. Who would do that?' He snapped his fingers. 'No one but the man who hired Sutterfield in the first place!'

'You mean that guy, Rizzo?' Cliff queried.

'Rizzo's a marionette on a string; he does whatever Lariquett tells him to do. This counterfeit trial? Paid stooges and hiring Deloss? It bespeaks of the top dog's strategy – Lariquett.'

'Yes, Jared,' Crystal allowed, her mind seeking answers. 'We've figured he was the guilty party from the start. But, how has anything changed . . . other than Sutterfield is now free as a bird? How do we get justice for what he did?'

Jared turned deadly serious. 'Sutterfield is living out his last hours, little lady. He hasn't answered for defaming my cousin's name and our family honor. Plus, I promised you the man is going to pay the full price for killing your brother. I always keep my promises.'

'Yes, except. . . .'

He held up his hand to stop her question or observation. 'I want you two to see the town, do some shopping, have a couple of good meals, then get a good night's sleep at the hotel.'

'What are you going to do in the meantime?' Cliff wanted to know.

'I'll be around,' he evaded. 'If everything works out, we will take the early train back to Boulder tomorrow.'

'But, Jerry. . . ?' Crystal began.

He leaned over, planted a brotherly kiss on her forehead, then showed her a confident smile. 'Trust me, Crystal. Everything is going to work out fine.'

Surprisingly, Crystal rewarded him with a timorous simper of her own. 'I do trust you, Jerry. Nothing you've said makes any sense to me, but we'll do as you say.'

Deloss Reed hummed the music to an off-color ditty as he removed his hat and jacket. It had been a good day. The money he earned for defending a two-bit gunman would keep him in comfort for several months. A few more well-paying clients and he would buy himself a house, instead of renting a room at this rundown boarding house.

He sat down on his bed and began to remove his shoes. The fullness of his stomach made it difficult to bend over, reminding him not to celebrate with such an excess of food and wine. He chuckled at the notion. How could anyone not enjoy the fruit of his success, along with the company of compliant female companions? What good was money, if a man didn't. . . .

'Don't move too sudden,' an icy voice hissed in his ear,

'or the knife at your throat will cut off your weasel head!'

Feeling a sharp blade at his Adam's apple, Deloss froze like a statue. He felt the weight of the man who had knelt down on the bed behind him. 'W-what do you want?' he stammered fearfully. 'Who are you?'

'You are going to answer one question for me,' the indistinguishable voice commanded. 'You lie . . . you die!' The man snickered, 'That should be simple enough for a lying jackal like you to understand.'

'How did you get in my room?'

The knife drew tighter against his throat. He feared it would break the skin.

Deloss lifted his hands out away from his body in a sign of total submission. 'Wait!' he whimpered. 'Don't hurt me!'

'You don't ask questions,' the intruder told him coldly. 'You answer them!'

'Yes, yes,' Deloss whimpered, now trembling from head to foot. 'What is the question?'

'Who hired you to produce those four drunks for the hearing today? I want the name of the man who paid you.'

'I don't know what you mean,' Deloss began. 'I was defending a client. I didn't—'

A hard rap on the side of his head stung his ear, causing him to nearly fall over. The knife remained in place, piercing the skin enough for it to bleed.

'Hold on!' he wailed. 'I'll tell you!'

'The next words from your mouth better be a name,' the deadly voice warned, 'or you are going to choke on your own blood!'

Jared arrived to stand alongside Cliff and Crystal on the

platform, waiting to board the train. Before either of them could ask where he'd been most of the night, Sergeant Fielding arrived and marched up to the trio. He did not have a happy look on his face.

'I know you did it!' Fielding declared loudly, pointing his finger at Jared. 'Don't lie to me – admit it!'

'You come to see us off, Sarge?' Jared ignored the accusation. 'I'm moved by your genuine concern.'

'Don't give me any hogwash, Valeron,' he snarled, obviously not in a good mood. 'Sutterfield turned up dead this morning. Seems he drank himself to death! Three bottles of rot-gut whiskey were found next to his body!'

Jared shook his head. 'Man shouldn't celebrate escaping a noose to the point of drinking that much booze.'

'Don't you dare tell me you had nothing to do with his death!'

'Glad to oblige,' Jared quipped, not responding to his allegation. 'Anything else you wanted?'

Fielding opened his mouth, then clamped it shut. With a shake of his head, he growled, 'Deloss Reed filed a report about an intruder last night, too. Said some spook was in his room and nearly removed his head with a large skinning knife.'

Jared snorted, 'I didn't bring a hunting knife with me, Fielding. I know how touchy you are about people carrying weapons on the Denver streets.'

The sergeant looked ready to pull out his own hair. 'You promised me, Jared! Now Sutterfield is dead!'

'I promised you I wouldn't force the man into a gunfight. Turns out, the coward was too frightened to touch his gun.'

'Then you admit you killed him?'

'No way,' he replied. 'We toasted to his health and good fortune . . . for several hours. I warned him it wasn't safe to drink so much whiskey, but he just kept on guzzling. When he finally passed out, I didn't feel like drinking alone, so I left.'

'Like I'm supposed to believe that.'

'I swear to you. . . .' Jared lifted his right hand, 'the man was still breathing when I left him.'

'But so full of rot-gut you knew he wouldn't survive!' Fielding growled.

'Don't fault me for the lowlife's lack of good sense.'

'The man shot and killed my brother in cold blood,' Crystal chastened the lawman. 'If Jerry had given me my gun, I would have gladly shot the miserable snake myself.'

'What about the lawyer?' Fielding threw the accusation at Jared. 'You can't sneak into a man's room and terrorize him.'

'Don't know what you're talking about, Sarge. I just admitted to spending most of the night toasting Sutterfield's health. Maybe someone else has a grudge against him.'

'You going to arrest Jared?' Cliff wanted to know.

Fielding lowered his head in defeat. 'No, I'm going to fill out two reports. One will concern an accidental death from too much cheap booze. The second will be an open case, with intruder unknown . . . but only because I'd like to see Deloss run out of town on a rail.'

'He'll probably end up as a senator or congressman,' Jared replied dryly.

'All aboard!' came a shout for those riding the train.

'That's us, Sarge,' Jared said easily. 'Anything else we can do for you?'

Fielding grunted. 'Just one thing.'

'Name it,' Jared offered.

'If you can't stay out of trouble, Valeron . . . at least, stay out of Denver!' And, with those words of farewell, he did an about-turn and stomped off.

The three of them found a seat on the train, but Crystal paused to throw her arms around Jared's neck. She hugged him tightly before sitting down.

'You should have told me what you were up to,' she scolded him. 'You knew I wanted to see Sutterfield get his due. I owed it to Donny.'

'He was a yellow skunk with a gun, Crystal. He didn't care who your brother was, he killed him for a wad of money.'

'Then that's it?' Cliff asked. 'We got the lowly private, while the general gets away ordering the actual murder?'

'Not exactly,' Jared said. 'Knowing for certain who is behind Donny's death doesn't help much if we can't prove it. If this were a game of cards, I would say we are down to our last hand,' he directed his words to Crystal. 'However, I've been holding back an ace.' With a sigh of resignation, he told them: 'It's time I played that ace . . . and hope no one trumps it.'

'Talk sense, Jared,' Crystal complained. 'Who or what is your ace?'

'I'm sorry, little lady, but this is something I will have to do privately.'

'Sounds dangerous,' Cliff chimed in. 'You want some back-up?'

Jared grunted. 'What I need is a sense of tact I've never had.'

As Cliff and Crystal stared at him with open confusion,

he leaned against the window and tipped his hat over his eyes.

'Wake me when we get to the train station.'

CHAPTER TWELVE

Rizzo entered the office unannounced as usual. Lariquett was sitting behind his desk, browsing through the latest edition of the Saturday Evening Post. He groaned at seeing the distressed mien on his friend's face.

'Tell me,' he muttered, prepared for the worst.

'You 'member, way back to yesterday, when I told you that Deloss got Sutter off?'

'Of course. I knew a shyster like him could do the job. What about it?'

'Sutter is dead.'

Lariquett dropped the magazine and stood up. 'Dead? How?'

'Drank himself to death . . . so says the telegraph message. Found him in his room with several empty whiskey bottles.'

'Goes to show, you should never give a drunk more than the price of a drink or two.'

'It gets worse.'

Lariquett heaved a sigh. 'What else?'

'Some night prowler done got inside the lawyer's room. Deloss said the intruder wanted information – namely, who hired him to defend Sutter.'

Lariquett balled his fists. 'And, it goes without saying, Deloss spilled his guts.'

'Can't be no doubt – Valeron is going to come for us.'

'Nothing we've done puts us in the sights of Valeron's gun,' Lariquett went over their defense.

'Sutterfield was a friend of yours. No one ever questioned you personally about him. I did you a favor by arranging his defense, but it was only because the man had done a little money-earning chore for us. The killing of Donny Duval is still a mystery. We didn't know anything about it before – we know nothing about it now.'

'You're sharp as a nail point, Chief,' Rizzo praised that line of reason. 'Sutter killed the bookkeeper on a whim, just for fun. It had nothing to do with us or the reason we hired him.'

'No motive, no crime.'

Rizzo skewed a worried frown. 'All the same, we ought to be ready.'

'Keep the boys on watch. If Valeron does come at us, we want to be ready.'

'I'm with you one hundred per cent,' Rizzo assured Lariquett.

'Prepared and protected,' Lariquett voiced his new motto.

'Let's make sure we don't get any surprises.'

Finding Sutterfield had been a no-brain chore. Managing to sneak inside the lawyer's room, that had required stealth and patience. But this . . . facing someone he knew very little about and understood even less? Adding to the problem, it had to be discreet.

To that end, Jared approached the elderly woman while she was outside tending to a small flower garden. She looked up when he moved to within a few feet of her.

'Mr Valeron,' Coleen said softly. 'Whatever are you doing here?'

'I need to speak to your sister-in-law, ma'am,' he did not waste words on proprieties. 'Privately.'

Coleen had not been a bad-looking woman. However, her near-fifty years had taken its toll; that much showed within the depths of her haunted eyes. Whether she had ever loved and lost, or never loved at all, it was hidden beneath a veneer of calm and courtesy.

'I'm not aware of Sylvia's interest in such an assignation.'

Jared chuckled. 'I do believe that's the first time I ever heard that word said aloud. I always shied away from using the word rendezvous, cause it seemed too intimate for polite conversation.'

His reply brought a smile to her face. 'I begin to think I misjudged you. When you entered my brother's office by knocking down and humiliating Rex, I assumed you were a bully with a gun.'

'I didn't want to hurt him,' Jared excused his behavior.

'Then,' Coleen continued on with her original summation, 'When Sylvia invited you to dine with us, I was pleasantly surprised at your display of manners.'

'Mom and my two aunts are responsible for that,' he confessed.

'Now, word has spread that the man who killed Donny Duval has died . . . while you and Miss Duval happened to be in the same city.' She eyed him with an odd scrutiny. 'You seem to me an enigma, Mr Valeron, but. . . .' she held up a hand to stop him from replying. 'But,' she began again, 'I am willing to help in any way I can.'

He smiled. 'You've a real polite way of circling the wagons before lighting down to make a stand.'

She laughed. 'And your metaphor is equally charming.'

'So, can you help me get a few minutes alone with Mrs Adour?'

'We are to dine shortly. If I were to make a picnic lunch for the two of us, it is probable we would end up down by the creek in approximately one hour. There's a place at the bend that is far enough away from town that only the occasional fisherman visits. It will grant you the privacy you need, but I must remain close enough to keep an eye on Sylvia. She is my responsibility, you understand.'

'I understand perfectly. I will be at the creek bend in exactly one hour.'

Jared walked away to discover Crystal had been watching from her upstairs window and saw him talking to Miss Adour. She met him at the door to the store with her hands placed neatly on her hips. She studied him with a curious frown.

'Why are you talking to Sylvia's sister-in-law?' she wanted to know. 'What are you up to?'

'It's part of the plan.'

'What plan?' she voiced her frustration. 'The man who killed my brother is dead, but we still don't know why Sutter wanted Donny dead!'

'All in good time, little lady.'

'And talking to Coleen Adour is part of your plan?'

'No, talking to Sylvia Adour is the plan.'

Crystal gave her head a negative shake. 'What on earth could Sylvia tell us that will help to find a motive?'

'Maybe nothing,' Jared admitted. 'It's a hunch.'

'A hunch,' she repeated. 'Was it a hunch that you could force Sutterfield to drink himself to death?'

'More or less.'

'What about the hunch that you could get away with entering a lawyer's home in the middle of the night and terrorizing answers out of him?'

'I suppose you could call it a hunch.'

'Jerry,' she expressed firmly, 'I never want to go fishing or hunting with you. I suspect one of your hunches would get us stuck in the middle of a hostile Indian camp!'

Lariquett glowered at Rizzo. 'You were supposed to be watching them!'

'There's only three of us and four of them – not counting the girl,' Rizzo excused the oversight. 'I stopped to check for any news at the telegraph office, while Keogh was watching the young Valeron. Blade was keeping track of Mitch and the one called Cliff . . . but they separated. Mitch headed for the livery, so he thought he ought to stick with him.'

'And Jared Valeron?'

'I was on him until I stopped to speak to Parker. Never could find him after that, not until he and Crystal showed up together on the street.'

'And now?'

'I don't know. The two of them entered the hardware store. A while later Crystal came out to meet with Mitch. It looked as if Cliff and the younger Valeron were gonna do the same.' He made a face, 'There was no sign of Jared himself. He slipped off on his own again.'

'Oh, that's just great. You and the boys are keeping

track of everyone except the one man who can hurt us the most. Jared is the brains of that bunch! He's the one we have to worry about!'

'Sorry, Chief. The guy is like one of those carnival magicians, he ups and disappears any time he wants.'

'OK, OK,' Lariquett simmered. 'It may look like we're too interested if we watch them all the time. Plus, it's obvious the three of you can't watch four people at once.'

'I don't like it,' Rizzo's anxiety surfaced. 'Why are the Valerons sticking around? I mean, they got Sutter, even after we cleared his name. He's the one they came for, the one who killed Donny Duval and pretended to be Wyatt Valeron. Why ain't they going home?'

'It's a mystery all right.' Lariquett rubbed his hands together thoughtfully. 'I can think of only one reason for their staying and it isn't one I like.'

'They couldn't possibly know you ordered Donny's death, Chief. No one knows that but the two of us.'

'Sutter could have talked.'

'It's like I told you before, Sutter didn't know nuthen! He was in hog heaven to get a thousand dollars to kill a man. He didn't ask why.'

'But you are tied to him, Rizzo.'

'Valeron ain't asked me one single question, not about nuthen!'

'Regardless of questions, he certainly knows you were involved.'

'You think he'll come gunning for me, Chief?'

'The man knows you work for me. He will assume I knew about Donny, whether I gave the order or not.'

'What'll we do?'

'Let's give them a day or two. If they decide to leave

town, this will be over.' At Rizzo's nod, he outlined: 'For the time being, keep the boys here at the saloon. If we have even an inkling they are going to come looking for us. . . .'

He didn't have to finish. 'I'll have them ready. If they look cross-eyed at us, they will be pushing up dirt with the toes of their boots.'

The sun was shining brightly and it was quite warm. Sylvia Adour arrived at the meeting place with a lace parasol over her shoulder. Coleen had accompanied her, but stopped a tactful distance away, where she could keep an eye out for any passersby.

Jared touched the brim of his hat in a salutatory welcome and smiled. 'I wasn't certain you would show, Mrs Adour. This could outwardly appear to be scandalous.'

She returned a pleasant simper. 'I pegged you for an honorable man, Mr Valeron. Otherwise, I would have sent my regrets.'

Jared had thought to provide a blanket for the lady to sit on. Once she had settled in place, he sat cross-legged on the opposite side, leaving a modest space between them. To his relief, Sylvia opened the conversation with a confession.

'I believe I know why you asked for this meeting.' Sobering with her admission, she lowered her eyes. 'You seem to be an intuitive man, and I'm aware of the trip you and Crystal made to Denver.'

'The attorney who defended Donny Duval's killer was hired by Lariquett,' Jared outlined. 'It confirms he is behind her brother's murder.'

'Yes, I too believe it was his doing.'

Jared uttered the next words as gently as he could. 'It also means Lariquett had a motive for being rid of Donny.'

She appeared to be frozen, not even taking a breath.

'I hate to ask you this, Mrs Adour,' he kept his voice as gentle as he could, 'but do you know the reason why Lariquett would order the death of his own bookkeeper?'

The lady exhaled the breath she'd been holding, swallowed hard, and refused to make eye contact. After several deep breaths, she began to speak. It was little more than a whisper and her voice was thick with emotion.

'Andrew is a womanizing lecher,' she began. 'He sees every woman as a potential trophy for his monumental ego. The fact that I married a man so much older than myself, he naturally assumed I would be interested in him. I must have put him off a dozen times in the past, but he kept coming back.'

She paused once more, her pained expression showing every word was ripped from her very soul. When she continued, a chill came into her words, frigid with ire, yet full of regret.

'Jacques went to Boulder to meet with our banker. He does so every month or two. I usually make the trip with him and Coleen and we do some shopping. However, Coleen was feeling poorly, so we stayed behind.'

She paused, as if to summon a reserve of courage, and proceeded with her narration. 'Mr Frye was doing the end-of-the-month reports and was missing the last week's figures from Donny. I offered to step over and collect the needed statements so he could keep working.'

Her aplomb waned, replaced by a tightening of her jaw and an icy tone hardening her voice. 'Mr Lariquett had been drinking . . . a lot. He stopped me before I reached

Donny's work room and literally dragged me into his office.

'I knew at once he was drunk and tried to scream, but he covered my mouth and attacked me. I physically tried to fight him off, but he is much stronger than me and was very determined. He forced me down on his desktop...' she swallowed a sob, '. . . and pinned me beneath his weight.' She took a breath and forced the next words to surface. 'I cursed him and struggled with all my might, while he slobbered over me, trying to kiss me.' Another pause, and regret filled her voice. 'That's when Donny opened the door.'

Tears began to slide down her cheeks. 'I don't think Donny saw much of anything, only Andrew leaning over an unwilling woman. He muttered a quick apology and the door closed again. Andrew was furious at the interruption, but it allowed me to escape from his clutches.'

'The filthy swine!' Jared rasped, filled with an unbridled rage.

'Andrew didn't try to grab me a second time, but he warned me to keep my mouth shut. He swore if I ever spoke of his actions, he would kill Jacques.' She looked up at Jared finally, tears glistening in her eyes. 'I didn't expect him to kill Donny. The young man didn't even know I was the woman being held down on the desk. But two days later, Donny was murdered on the street.' She violently shook her head. 'I believe Andrew was sending me a message – showing me that Jacques's life was in my hands.'

Jared reached over and rested his hand on her forearm. Never comfortable trying to console a woman, he did give it his best effort.

'None of this is your fault, Mrs Adour,' he told her

gently. 'Things happen beyond our control, it's a part of life. You can't blame yourself for being the victim of an attack, or for Donny's death; that is all on Lariquett.'

'But I kept silent.'

'You came to me,' he reminded her. 'You didn't have to risk being seen with me, allowing me to share dinner with you and Coleen. I know you've been trying to help me, ever since my arrival. I'm sorry that I couldn't get enough evidence to bring down Lariquett without this private meeting. But, the truth is, I couldn't act until I discovered the man's motive for killing Donny.'

'And now that you know the truth?'

He mustered an inexorable grin. 'You don't have to worry about protecting your secret, or your husband. In fact, Jacques best start looking for someone new to run the saloon.'

Lariquett was counting the money from the safe. It things suddenly turned sour, he intended to have a bag ready to go. It wouldn't be the fortune he had hoped for – too much money had been spent on keeping his botched attempt to seduce Sylvia a secret. A thousand dollars to Sutter, another thousand to Deloss for bribes and his fee, plus actually putting down the money for the new roulette wheel and other equipment. It had about cleaned out his stash. Now, with Valeron breathing down his neck, he had to be. . . .

Rizzo burst through the door, panting like a hunting dog that had tried to run down a deer. He gulped down some air and threw his hands in the air.

'We are in it now!' he gasped. 'Keogh saw Sylvia and Coleen taking a stroll down to the creek with a basket lunch a bit ago.'

'So what?' Lariquett demanded, wondering about his state of panic. 'They often have a picnic lunch.'

'Yeah, but five minutes after they returned from the stream, he seen Valeron come from the same direction. I'll wager he was at the picnic, too!'

Lariquett's stomach roiled like he had swallowed a river rat whole and it was trying to escape. The shock of what a clandestine meeting meant caused his knees to weaken until he could barely stand.

'Whadda' you think?' Rizzo ranted. 'They shore didn't meet to do a little spooning behind old man Adour's back, not with his sister in tow!'

'No,' he lamented, 'Besides which, Sylvia's one of those honorable women who takes her wedding vows to heart. Is there anything else?'

'The younger Valeron headed down to the train station. I reckon he's leaving for some reason.'

Lariquett did some quick thinking. 'I would guess he is going to get warrants for our arrest.'

Rizzo was stunned. 'Warrants? What happened to our alibi, the story we had ready for. . . .'

'Trust me,' he said thickly. 'We only have one option now. And we must act quickly.'

'What's the plan, Chief?' Rizzo asked between breaths. 'Is it time to fight or run?'

From somewhere deep inside, the urge to strike back overruled Lariquett's desire to escape. That damn Valeron had ruined everything. And the foundation of this downfall – one lousy indiscretion! He could have laughed at the cynical, ridiculous notion – he hadn't even gotten a decent kiss!

'Jared is the only real threat. The other two don't look so tough.' He snorted, 'Hell, the one still here is wearing a belt buckle that says Daddy on it. If the other Valeron left town, it only leaves Jared and the daddy. Two of them won't be a match for you three,' Lariquett summed up the situation. 'Get it done, Rizzo, before they have a chance to move against us. Tell the boys it's time to earn their hired-gun pay.'

'What about Mitch and the girl?'

'Mitch won't do anything on his own. He and his brother aren't fighters.'

'Crystal Duval ain't one you can reason with,' Rizzo warned. 'She went gunning for Wyatt Valeron!'

'Once Valeron and the other one are being fitted for coffins by the undertaker, we will take what money we have and get the hell out of here.'

'OK, Chief. Sounds like you've got all the angles covered. I'll grab the boys and we'll see about making them two dead real sudden!'

'Do it right now, before that third Valeron returns or Jared has time to execute his own plan.'

Rizzo waved his understanding, rushing out the door. The time had come – kill Valeron and his cousin, or be killed by them!

CHAPTER THIRTEEN

Jared had feared someone might have seen him returning from his meeting with Sylvia. Lariquett's men had been taking turns keeping an eye on him and Cliff ever since they arrived. He cursed his carelessness at not taking a longer route back to town.

He first rushed to visit Shane at the rooming house. His job had been to keep an eye during the night, so he had caught up on his sleep during the day. To conform with Brett's wishes, Jared decided to do everything according to the rules. That mean sending Shane to get a couple of warrants for Rizzo and Lariquett. Having met with the Boulder policeman, Mylan Kochever, before coming to Quick-Silver, he felt certain the man would get him those warrants.

Shane had to hurry to catch the train, and would be back on tomorrow morning's train.

Rather than involve Crystal and Mitch, he avoided going to see either of them. Instead, he took to the back alleys and used the shadows to stay out of sight. He wanted to keep everyone safe until they were ready to move against Lariquett.

He knew Crystal was up in her apartment. She'd said something about washing her hair. Mitch had to handle some blacksmith work and would be with his brother at the livery. So that left only Cousin Cliff to warn and protect.

The question of where Cliff might be was answered a few moments later. He came walking down the street, having been visiting with the Winters boys at the black-smith workshop. Jared broke from cover and started out to meet him. He had only taken a few steps when a woman's cry split the serene quiet.

'Jared! Look out!' Crystal's voice came from her apart-ment window. 'It's a trap!'

Cliff made the mistake of looking up towards Crystal, who was pointing at three armed men. Before he had time to turn that direction, gunfire erupted. Cliff grabbed his left side and went down to his knees. To keep from offer-ing up a larger target, he fell forward on to his chest and snaked his right hand down to get his gun.

Jared was already moving forward. He drew and fired at the first shooter he saw – the man folded in the middle. But the attention of the remaining ambushers turned on him. Two bullets screamed past his body, while a third kicked up dirt at his feet. He got a second gunman in his sights and sent two well-placed slugs into his upper torso. That's when something slammed into the top of his left shoulder, near the base of his neck.

Stunned for a second, he saw Rizzo had taken the shot. The gunman left his concealment and started moving towards Jared like a madman, pulling the trigger again and again. One bullet went through the side of Jared's shirt, but another hit his right thigh, causing him to fall to the ground. He kept hold of his gun and rolled over, trying to avoid Rizzo's rain of lead.

Cliff recovered enough to get into the game, twisting sideways to bring his gun to bear. He fired three times at Rizzo and one scored a hit near the man's temple. Rizzo's gun flew from his fist as he slumped downward and spilled onto his back.

Jared held his gun ready, but the scrap seemed to be over. He got to his feet and glanced at Cliff. His cousin waved that he was OK but out of the fight. With his left hand against the lower neck wound, Jared dragged his one injured leg and headed for the saloon. He knew the fight would only be finished when the head man was dead or had surrendered. With a grim determination, he entered through the bat-wing doors.

From the street, he heard Crystal yell: 'Jared! Wait!' But he bulled ahead, gun in hand, searching the casino and bar area for Lariquett. He watched the upstairs, thinking the man might come out of his office, but he had let his fury control his actions. He should have been more cautious.

'Got you!' Lariquett sounded off gleefully from where he had been hiding.

As Jared turned, a lead missile rammed high into his right arm. It knocked the gun from his hand and he went down onto his one good knee. He grimaced from the pain of his third bullet wound and looked up . . . completely helpless, as the saloon owner flashed a triumphant sneer.

'Took down my best friend and his two men,' Lariquett snarled his contempt. 'But you're my meat now, Valeron. Here's where you die!'

Two shots resounded off of the walls.

Jared stared at the muzzle of Lariquett's gun, awaiting the bright flash and hot lead that would end his life.

It didn't come.

Lariquett pitched forward and landed flat on his face. Behind him, a tendril of smoke still rising from her gun, Crystal strode up to the man's body. Looking down at him, she spat on his dying body.

'I know you ordered Donny killed,' she cried. 'I swore I would get the man responsible.'

'And,' Jared added through teeth gnashed in pain, 'I'm damned glad you did!'

She hurried over to him and sank down to her knees. 'Good Lord, Jerry,' she declared. 'You've got more holes in you than a pin cushion. Didn't you try to duck any of the bullets?'

'I'll live,' he replied. 'Thanks to you, little lady. Your timing was perfect.'

Crystal, Mitch and Shane met Nash and Trina with luminous smiles as they entered the hospital lobby in Boulder.

'Your brother is a terrible patient,' were Crystal's words of greeting to Nash. 'He kept telling the doctors he wanted to wait for you to treat his wounds. They finally had to knock him out with chloroform to patch him up.'

'I can believe it,' Nash replied. 'He broke his finger one time when helping brand some cattle. Biggest baby I ever dealt with.'

'The doctors here have a good reputation. It's why we got them here as quickly as possible.'

'How's Cliff?'

'His wound was the worst. The bullet took a piece of

rib, but the doctor said it should heal all right.'

'Who's the fellow at your elbow,' Trina asked.

Shane did the honors, 'Meet Mitch Winters. He has been helping Jerry from the beginning.'

'I'm not much good with a gun,' Mitch admitted. 'Besides which, by the time I knew there was a shootout on the main street of town, it was over.' He tipped his head at Crystal, 'My girl here, she was the hero of the gunfight.'

As Crystal didn't object to him calling her his girl, neither Nash nor Trina mentioned it. Instead, they followed after the trio, making their way down a hallway to several patient rooms. They entered a cubicle with two beds – occupied by Cliff and Jared. Both were awake and cognizant.

Trina was the first to speak to the wounded men. 'You were supposed to look out for Cliff!' she directed her scolding at Jared. 'He's a father!'

'Actually, he looked after me,' Jared told her. 'In fact, he and Crystal took turns saving my hide.'

'They might have saved it, but it sounds as if you were both used for target practice. How many times were you hit?'

Jared grunted, 'Only a nick here or there, until a bullet in my right arm put me out of the game.'

'I took one through my ribs, Nash,' Cliff tossed in his ante. 'My belt buckle stopped a round that would have ended my days.'

'Gaudy as it is, you'll have to thank Nessy for buying it for you,' Jared reminded him.

Cliff grinned, 'Sneaky little twerp, she had Darcy order it from the store – came all the way from back east.'

Nash took time to inspect Cliff's injury. 'Crystal was

right,' he announced. 'It looks as if the doctor did a fine job.'

Trina stood at Jared's side, peeling back his bandages for a look. 'These look good too,' she said. 'Now then, are you going to tell us how you both ended up shot?'

Jared sighed. 'How about I go straight to my playing Cupid? I helped promote a romance between Crystal and the blacksmith.'

Mitch bobbed his head in agreement. 'Gave me a push in the right direction. I'd always been too standoffish to tell Crystal how I felt.'

'I knew he was interested,' Crystal admitted. 'But I had about given up on him ever trying to court me proper.'

Jared popped off again. 'Add to that, Trina – I also protected the good name of a faithful wife.'

'What about Cliff and Crystal each saving your life?' Nash asked his brother.

'Hardly worth mentioning,' Jared joked. 'Cliff got in a lucky shot. As for Crystal, I took care of the guy who killed her brother. It's only fair she should put an end to the guy who hired the job done.'

'We'll leave these two wounded heroes in your care,' Crystal said to Nash. 'Mitch and I have to get back to Quick-Silver. The train leaves in less than an hour.'

'If I don't get back for the wedding,' Jared cracked, 'be sure to name one of your kids after me.'

'I'm not fond of the name "Trouble",' Crystal laughed.

'And twins would made the second born "Double Trouble",' Mitch joined in. 'Not really the namesakes we want – especially if the kids turn out to be girls.'

Trina and Nash laughed as Jared turned to look at Cliff.

'See what I've been telling you? This hero business

never really does pan out.'

'Yep,' his cousin replied. 'You won't have to remind me not to join you the next time you get in over your head. Being a hero's comrade ain't much better!'